The Gospel of
Wolves

Ep. 1

❖

Chris Wesley

The Mining Town of Charlemagne, Colorado is loosely based on Gilman, Colorado.

Front Cover Design by: J Caleb Clark
www.jcalebdesign.com

COPYRIGHT 2014 Chris Wesley

ISBN: 978-0-9846754-1-8

First Book Edition - July 2014.

10 9 8 7 6 5 4 3 2 1

Published by Artistic Agenda Press
2271 Lake Avenue
P.O. Box 6604

The Gospel of Wolves takes place approximately:

* 14 years before *The Pilgrimage Vignettes:*
    * *Husk*
    * *Hotel Arrianda*
    * *If Blood Were Breadcrumbs*

* 14 years before *Regret in Triptych.*

For more info on The Wilderness Saga and the variety of media the story is told in, visit:
www.chriswesley.com/media

CONTENTS

Andros Koresh
(Friday, 15 December 2006)

The first dream I ever watched die looked to have a long future ahead of it. It belonged to Evan Wilkie, who reminded me of a Caucasian version of L.L. Cool J because of the Kangol hat he always kept his shaved head covered with. At the time we met, his dream was to be a film director, and if you paid attention, you would notice that he had a sharpness behind his gaze, as if he was always processing what his eyes were taking in and mentally framing the composition of objects and people into a sixteen by nine sized window into their lives.

Evan and I were both at a cafe in Hollywood that adored painting everything black and catered to independent filmmakers with book racks full of scripts from popular movies for sale. The idea was that you could study them or model your own script after their structure. There was also a small library of technical books geared towards the many different roles that scroll across the screen while people brush popcorn out of their laps to make for the exit.

Along with 16 other people, we were occupying one of several different rooms that could be reserved for meetings like the one that brought Evan and I together. It was a read through and crew huddle for an indie movie about a girl in her late teens looking for love and identity while suffering from a mild mental disability, called Millicent.

Introductions were made all around the large table and I felt that brief sense of a team, newly formed, and hungry for a common goal. As soon as the actors had finished reading through the script and received their call sheets with our schedule and locations however, the talent bugged out so they could enjoy the rest of their day, while us crew talked logistics and took inventory of our equipment.

Evan was doing the cinematography and I was doing sound, so we spent extra time working out how we would use less than ideal equipment to capture sight and sound from seven different locations including four outdoor sites throughout Los Angeles without film permits. Among our challenges was doing this in a way that would avoid Police confiscation while giving the writer/director Warren Harpool what he needed to edit and release the short film.

By the time we wrapped Millicent three weeks later, and in spite of the many on-set arguments between Evan and 'One Take Warren', as Evan described him, it was easy to imagine Evan making his living directing movies based on what I saw him bring to the set each day. He understood not just where to point the camera and how to frame an interesting shot, but he was also able to coax subtle elements of character out of the actors that hinted at back stories Warren wasn't always able to.

I suppose that's why it was such a shock to me when months had passed after Millicent had wrapped without Evan taking on any new directing or cinema photography gigs. Instead, he alternated between background acting in hopes of qualifying for a Screen Actors Guild membership and transporting items as a courier for companies who needed an actual person to escort documents and other items to places like Thailand and Vietnam. He used the courier job as a means of cheap travel and often suggested that I do the same, but after hearing his tales of being robbed and enduring troubles with tarantulas during some of his trips, I didn't see the bargain he did.

He and I still hung out every now and then though, usually meeting to catch up at a Pasadena burger joint he liked. A year post Millicent, he suggested that he swing by my place so he could show me his demo reel in hopes that I would help him record new foley sound effects for it. At first, I thought he was finally going to pursue directing, but he corrected my enthusiastic support of that goal with an admonishing, "I'm trying to get a job at an advertising firm."

Over the course of our friendship, he had grown increasingly sour on the notion of directing feature films and I could see why he wasn't finding the gigs he wanted after he showed me his demo reel. He had a stylized vision that hearkened back to the classic days of film noir with the stark and mysterious airs you would expect to find Humphrey Bogart breathing in with a wit every bit as precisely aimed as the pistol you knew he had waiting beneath his suit coat.

"The last time I tried to get a job with an advertising firm, they told me that this look isn't selling these days," Evan said.

I saw his point, but also saw what could be a defining style. If he married it to the right script, he could have enjoyed some play in movie theaters and if the issue of a movie filmed in black and white was too large to overcome, I saw how muted colors against vivid whites and reds could help him over that hump. Evan dismissed my thoughts though, with the kind of "Nah," I might have been given if I had offered him a drink when he wasn't thirsty.

When I questioned him about creating his own project like Warren had done with Millicent, Evan complained about Warren's finished product and veered around my actual question until I tired of rephrasing it. I did agree to help him create some new sound effects for his demo reel though, because it was obvious how well developed his eye was, even if the shooting style wasn't trending in the advertising world at that moment.

After sending his reel out to prospective employers, the silence he predicted from the agencies turned prophetical. Three months in to his wait for a call back, I made the mistake of telling Evan about a movie I had seen a few days prior named Stomp Box. It was a summer blockbuster type of movie as heavy on action as it was light on storyline, but I was telling him how much I enjoyed it anyhow. The conversation quickly turned in a direction I hadn't anticipated when Evan interrupted me and said, "Dave Rikkum directed that. I hate Dave Rikkum. We went to film school together and he didn't like any of my projects. Don't talk to me about Dave Rikkum."

I didn't know what to say to that. I was equally speechless when he announced a few months later, that he was done. He was moving to Portland, Oregon because he was sick of Hollywood. We were on the phone, but I could see the expression that went with that tone of voice. That sense that he got the raw deal he always knew was waiting for him while others, like Dave Rikkum, brought in millions of dollars summer after summer with movies that relied on the sparkle of special effects rather than the substance of characters that reached into our chest cavities and made us feel something strong.

I made one last plea because I was scared and saddened by the defeat I heard in his voice, knowing it was futile, but believing it had to be said. I told him, "You failed to get a job selling soft drinks and toilet paper. You never really tried to direct feature films like you dreamed, at least not since I've known you, which means there's hope if you actually make a move on your goal." Then, I suggested again that he write a short film script that fit the tone of his vision for the look of the film, before casting and shooting the thing himself as a means of building a name for himself and growing his career from there like so many other writer/directors that had similar beginnings of looking for an audience rather than an open minded gatekeeper.

Two weeks later Evan was in Portland, taking yearbook pictures for the local junior high and high schools. Over the phone, he sounded as disinterested in life as I had ever heard from him, but I made no effort to put my mouth on the lips of that corpse and try to breathe life back into a dead dream.

I hadn't thought about him in a couple years, but I was hours away from flying up to Portland myself. Not on the wings of my own dream, but on those of his Plan B, the advertising and branding firm I worked for called Razor[Gun].

It was 15 minutes before midnight and I laid in bed debating whether it was wise or not to contact Evan while I was in town. In the background was the cackling of paper shopping bags as my temporary roommate and fellow dream chaser pulled things out of them in the other room. She was humming a melody that rode along top of the sound from the bags as she rummaged inside them and set the contents aside.

I tried to doze back off by focusing on the soft drone of the falling rain outside, but thirty minutes after we officially crossed into Friday morning, I gave up trying to sleep. The shopping bags had quieted, but were immediately replaced by a different clamor as she noisily moved about my apartment, now humming a different song.

I pulled myself out of bed and took residence in the hallway unnoticed for a few moments while watching her as she rearranged miniature ornaments on a three foot Christmas tree positioned on the floor near my apartment's front door. The tree had appeared while I was asleep along with the five or six wrapped presents surrounding the base of it, all too large to fit completely under it.

I quietly padded further into my living room and found two Christmas stockings hanging from the fireplace mantle. Both were stuffed full and had masking tape slapped across them. One had 'Puppy' written on the tape, the other had 'Tessa' written on it. Like the Christmas tree and presents, they were recent additions to my apartment.

"Puppy!" She said, finally noticing me and calling me by the nickname she gave me. "How do you like it?" She stood up and back, admiring her work on the Christmas tree and throughout the room as she waited for my praise.

"Where did you get all this?" I asked instead.

"Alma." She said, still elated and patient for the expected compliment. "We made up when I dropped off my key to the apartment. I told her what a Grinch you are and she gave me this stuff in hopes your heart will grow."

"That was nice of her," I said, "but I keep my heart bound in an iron casing to make sure it stays the size of a pea."

She smirked. "Are you still traveling tomorrow?" She asked as if it were still Thursday.

I leaned against the wall. "Yep."

"Do you want to pull out the guitar? We can work on a song while I finish decorating."

No. I didn't want to pull out the guitar. I wanted to go to sleep because between work and my time spent writing music with Tessa, I'd been averaging about three hours of sleep a night for the past few months and felt exhausted.

True, I was traveling for work in about seven hours, but that meant I needed to be capable of working after arriving at my destination and since we were shooting for a television campaign, I was expecting 18 hour days while we were up in Portland. I knew from experience however, that she'd eventually break down my resistance and I figured why waste the energy fighting when I knew I'd eventually comply. "Sure," I told her. Moments later, I was sitting on the couch, acoustic guitar in hand.

My best friend, Lindsey Falco liked to say that I had trouble saying no to pretty women and the fact that Tessa was only 18 only made things worse. "She isn't gorgeous, but she's pretty enough. If you can manage to make one decision out of ten with the head you're not worried about catching in a zipper, I'll be proud of you," she told me after meeting Tessa.

"Play something happy, but with an edge," Tessa said and I went through five minutes of head shaking and shrugs from her in response to the music I was producing before finally laying into a lively romp that had her swaying her hips to the rhythm as she took the stack of Christmas cards mailed to me by friends and family and tented them along the mantle to my fireplace. By the time she had all the cards on display, she was singing, "You know you can't fit this cookie in your glass, and the chocolate chips and walnuts are big and bad."

After a time, her words faded in my awareness, leaving only the tone of the mood created by the sass in her delivery and the syncopating strum I had pumping it along. My initial irritation and fatigue both evaporated as she and I pushed, prodded and pulled each other along, riding through an ever evolving landscape of emotions in sound. What began as something rough and hungry, resolved into light, tickling touches of flourish, teasingly stoking heat and anticipation until things got rowdy again and the raking of guitar pick across the metal strings of my guitar had grown into a furor so intense that I broke a string.

The fall that followed was like that moment without gravity as you crest the top of the rails on a coaster and begin your descent.

Tessa pulled loose, sweaty strands of hair out of her face. A smile crept like vines along the edges of her mouth. The glow of our combined chemistry was beginning to dissipate, but I wasn't ready to be finished yet. "Go again?" I asked, appetite still evident in my voice. "I can plug in my electric."

She shook her head. "I need a shower and a bed."

So did I. The 4:13 reading from my wall clock felt like an accusing stare. I had to start getting showered and dressed for my trip at six, so I skipped cleaning myself up for the moment and merely changed out of my wet sweats and t-shirt before climbing back in bed hoping that my adrenaline would power down while Tessa's humming echoed from the shower. The sound of the rain droning in the background puddled, then flowed into my consciousness until my drift off into slumber was complete.

***

I hadn't been out of the shower for ten minutes when the pounding on my front door started. It sounded like two different people begging an answer, but it turned out to only be Chaz Latham using both hands and the steel toe of one boot harassing the otherwise silent morning air.

In his former life, Chaz had gone from cinematographer on two feature length films to writer-director on six more before making the inexplicable switch to jack-of-filmed-trades for Razor[Gun]. For the job he and I were about to embark on, he was to direct a series of commercials we were shooting for Everain Beer, a microbrewery in Portland, Oregon that was quickly growing in national popularity and in need of a marketing identity.

"Travel day!" He said, smile as wide as the sky, as I opened the door, his demeanor in stark contrast to the violence in his knock.

"Yep," I agreed, not making any attempt to mirror his enthusiasm, but we both had accepted our differences in emotional amplitude.

He glided in to my apartment, grabbed my equipment case in one hand, my suitcase in the other and walked back out, leaving me no task but to lock up and follow. He led me to the car talking about some club he was hoping to hit while we were in Portland. "The Lackwits and Verse Eye are performing Saturday night, that means we can't be screwing around with these commercials."

I hadn't heard either of the artists he was talking about, but still told him, "Sounds good to me."

"You look like hell!" Our senior producer Jackie Strickland said as I climbed into the minivan.

"Well, I'm riding with the Devil," I shot back.

Her eyes narrowed at me enough for me to recognize the mistake in saying that and I apologized before throwing morning greetings at our cinematographer, Jeremy Mackie and our documentary filmmaker Araceli Diaz, who was tasked to film all the behind the scenes action and drama as we created for our clients.

The ride to Bob Hope Airport consisted mostly of Jackie going over details of the shoot, Chaz making a few remarks about the call schedules he had handed us, and then the sounds of hip-hop music as Chaz made sure we understood the significance of his getting to see Verse Eye while we were up north because Verse Eye was signed to an indie label and was only touring in the Pacific Northwest region.

Even though he wasn't technically in charge, Chaz didn't hesitate in navigating our entourage directly to the airport bar as soon as we cleared security, even though it was only seven in the morning.

"This is why we needed to get here early?" Jackie asked him. "I thought you were worried about lines through security."

"The vibe by which one starts a job, is the tone by which one either enjoys or endures said job," Chaz told her, then proceeded to take a very long pull from his beer. When he finally put the glass mug down, his eyes were closed in some kind of reverie and he had foam in his bushy mustache.

"You have a problem," Jackie told him.

Chaz' eyes remained closed. "It's people with problems who look at a clock before imbibing," he told her.

Jackie didn't look convinced, but knew that even though her job title technically outranked the lot of us during this trip, Chaz was a highly coveted hire and he'd have to just about nuke a Razor[Gun] office to get fired.

"C'mon Araceli, let's take a breather from the Y Chromosomes." She turned to Chaz. "We'll meet you three at the gate." Then she shot me a dirty look that gave me the feeling that calling her the Devil was a mistake I had yet to begin paying for.

Chaz, Jeremy and I, watched them walk in the direction of our gate. After they were out of earshot, Chaz asked me, "What's with the dark circles under your eyes? Jackie's right, you don't look well."

"I haven't been getting much sleep."

Chaz gave me a few seconds to say more, but when I didn't, told me, "Elaborate."

"I'm working with a singer. She met Rudy Ginger, the manager for The Palm Fronds and he might be willing to consider managing us and picking us up for the west coast portion of The Palm Fronds tour, but he wanted to hear everything we have recorded to see how developed we are. I'm also doing some merch and poster designs because the merch table is really where we'll be making our money. We won't be making much of anything off the actual performances."

Chaz radiated skepticism. "How long is this tour supposed to last?"

"A month. During that time, I'll be telecommuting my end of whatever projects Razor[Gun] has me live on at the time," I went on to tell him that I cleared the whole thing with our West Coast Regional Art Director, Rodrick Alexander, just in case Tessa and I could make the tour happen.

He nodded his head in a way that left me feeling like he meant to roll his eyes instead. "You sign a contract?"
"Not yet. Tessa passed Rudy a demo CD with a couple of our songs to see how he likes them, we should hear back in a day or two."

"Who's the singer again?"

"Tessa Carrillo."

"How'd you and this Tessa meet?"

"At a hostel in Santa Monica. She'd just come to California from her hometown of Charlemagne, Colorado to be a singer and I was there because they had a poetry open mic night. Some guy got on her about her poetry and I

17

defended her because we all had to start somewhere, and after that, she and I got to talking and hit it off. It helped some that she wants to sing and I have a project recording studio in the spare bedroom of my apartment."

Chaz took a pull from his beer, then, "How old is she?"

"18."

"Screwing her?"

"No!"

He gestured as if to ask what did I expect. "Had to ask."

"Look," he continued, "I know I come from the motion picture side of things, but the entertainment industry is the entertainment industry. Keep your head on a swivel, get things in writing and have an attorney that you hired yourself look over the contracts. Actually, before you hire the attorney, tell the attorney all the parties involved and ask him or her if there's a conflict of interests in representing you. You'd be amazed at the things I've seen."

"Is that why you got out of the industry?"

"Because I got screwed over?" He laughed at some private thought. "No. Although I did take it from the rear while on all fours from a few deals. My reasons for leaving were more personal and let's just leave it at that." Chaz looked at his watch. "We still have an hour before the plane boards, you should put your head down and get some rest."

I put my head down on the table and was asleep in seconds. I was dreaming that some guy almost ran me over in a car while I was crossing the street when Chaz shook me awake so we could go to our gate and board our flight. "Up and at 'em tour boy," he told me.

When we got to the gate, the plane was already boarding. As we approached, Jackie still looked angry and started talking loudly as soon as we were within ten yards of her. "You and Lindsey are friends, right? Outside of work?" She asked me.

The fact that Lindsey and I knew each other before I helped her get hired at Razor[Gun] was common knowledge. The details of our relationship were purposely vague, so I gave her a confused look for an answer because I didn't know where she was going with her question and wanted maneuvering room in case I had to play stupid over something Jackie didn't need to know.

Jackie attempted to wait me out and see what information I might volunteer, but her impatience over my silence got the better of her and she continued, "Any reason you can think of, why she isn't answering her phone? I just got off a call with Lyle and Colleen Everain who, by the way, also can't reach her and because of this, think it best that they should co-direct the five commercials that we're flying up to film. Since her name is at the top of their rant, Lindsey gets to clean this up."

I could have given Jackie a dozen reasons why Lindsey wouldn't take her call, but instead told her, "Maybe she's in the middle of something."

"What do you mean co-direct?" Chaz asked Jackie. "I'm not co-directing with two other people. Every decision turns into a discussion. We'll be there three weeks filming two and a half minutes worth of spots."

"You're right Chaz. You won't be co-directing with anyone. They want you to stay out of the way and let them fulfill their artistic vision." Jackie told him.

Chaz let out a contemptuous snort.

Jackie continued, "They claim the contract they signed with Razor[Gun] gives them the right to make this demand since they worked with Lindsey through this entire process until now."

A curse shot out of Chaz' mouth with enough anger to cause those within a few feet of him to back warily away from him.

"So everything I storyboarded is food for termites?" Jeremy asked.

"You'll shoot what they tell you unless Lindsey turns this around."

Jeremy sat down in a seat looking depressed.

"Call her," Jackie told me. "Call her family, her other friends, neighbors, anyone and keep dialing until you have her on the phone or they close the cabin door to the plane. Neither she, nor we, want this shoot being run by a couple home brewers with fantasies of creative genius."

Lindsey Falco
Friday, 15 December 2006

"Mommy. I don't think daddy's gonna make it."

It wasn't just what little Melanie said, it was how she said it that caused Lindsey to duck down to eye level with her daughter before reassuring her. "Don't be silly dear, your father will be here any moment to get us and we'll be on our way home."

Melanie didn't seem convinced. She appeared as if she was listening to someone who was telling her something she didn't want to hear. Whomever that some-one was, it wasn't her mother, Lindsey felt. She stayed down at eye level with Melanie a little while longer, brushed some of Melanie's bangs back under the hood of her coat, then stood upright and looked around the airport receiving area for her husband's car. They had been waiting for half and hour, but the airport was busy, and with the rain, there were surely traffic problems. She resisted the urge to pull out her cell phone and call him. After what Melanie said, Lindsey was afraid of doing any-thing that might encourage her that something really was wrong.

It seemed like half of the people driving had bought the exact same make, model, color and year of the car her husband owned. With the sky's reflection bouncing off of the windshields, the identities of the driv-ers remained concealed until they drove past her and

Melanie. Every single time, though, she held her frustration and impatience behind a veneer of calm that was becoming harder and harder to maintain each time she mistakenly thought she had spotted him.

If he doesn't come in the next five minutes, I'm calling him, Lindsey thought to herself. Knowing that this might upset Melanie further, Lindsey looked down to see how Melanie was fairing to gauge if she needed to provide any additional consoling before the call, but Melanie wasn't there. Lindsey glanced all around her immediate area, but her daughter was gone.

"Melanie!"

Looking to the parents of a family that had been standing next to them, she asked, "Did you see which way my daughter went? She's wearing a pink overcoat with the hood up and black stockings?"

Both of the parents gave a quick glance around, then offered sympathetic shrugs.

Lindsey forgot about her luggage and began pushing through the crowd of people yelling her daughter's name. The amount of people seemed to increase with Lindsey's anxiety and somehow, they seemed to always manage to be where she was trying to get to and move into the cracks and seams right as Lindsey attempted to peer through to catch a glimpse of where her daughter might be. Irritated by the mass of bodies, she tried stooping down to knee level thinking that looking between legs rather than around torsos might provide more gaps to peer through, but it was a moving forest of limbs that again seemed to move directly into her line of sight as quickly as she looked in a direction.

Realizing that there were too many people to get a clear view of someone her daughter's height, she stopped for a moment to think what the smartest thing to do was.

Making her decision, still yelling her daughter's name over the noise of the airport crowd, she pushed her way towards the street. She waited as a car pulled up to the curb and then she darted behind it and began running across the road. A car in the next lane had to swerve to avoid hitting her and the driver honked his horn. Lindsey ignored him, but held her palm out in the direction of oncoming traffic as she continued to race the rest of the way to the island on the other side. Once there, she turned back to the crowds hoping that from her new vantage point she might stand a better chance of seeing her daughter in spite of the crowded sidewalk.

The moments began to pile one on top of the other and the stress of their weight was beginning to fracture Lindsey's resolve. She realized that the longer it took to find her daughter, the less chance she had of recovering her. She cursed herself for not holding Melanie's hand as she attempted to stave off the belief that someone might have pulled her into their car and might, at that very moment, already be on the freeway to a location the police would never find. The tears were pushing their way up through their ducts as Lindsey dashed off of the curb passing a group of passengers crossing the street towards the self-parking garage. Once across, she began pushing her way through people again trying to get back to the area she first lost Melanie when someone grabbed her arm from behind.

Lindsey attempted to jerk free, but the grip was too powerful and as she recoiled back into the person, his other arm wrapped around her torso and pulled her into him. She felt her back bump up against his chest.

Out of trained reflex, she pulled her legs off of the ground, dropping her weight suddenly. Not wanting to get pulled down, her attacker loosened his grip.

Lindsey landed in a crouch, half turned to her left and with her left hand grabbed his belt to stabilize herself. Her training taught her that he would crouch down after her to grab at her a second time, so she began circling around his left leg. She slipped on the wet ground and it felt like something had tangled around her from the waist down, but she kept hold of his belt, pumping her legs to gain purchase and raise herself up. Off balance, she made her way slightly behind him as she felt his hands trying to grasp at her, she made a concerted push with her legs and pull on his belt to elevate herself just enough to plant her right fist into his left kidney.

His flesh didn't give the way she expected, though-it was harder than it should have been. Pain flashed from her closed fist. Everything went black. She consciously opened her eyes and realized they were already open.

Instinctively, she let go of his belt to use that hand

to pull off whatever was put over her head and fell to her knees. One hand shot to the ground to steady her balance while the other clasped empty air where she expected to find and tear off whatever had been placed over her head. Quickly, she sunk to the ground, attempting to roll away from her assailant and remain a moving target. The ground was soft and sagged beneath her movements. It felt to her like reality itself was beginning to bend around her and she was struggling to process what was happening when she fell over the side of something. The curb?

The small drop she expected from curb to street didn't happen.

Instead, she was airborne for at least twice as long as she should have been and landed hard enough for the ground to knock the air out of her lungs. The world brightened with a flash of white as her head smacked the ground a fraction of a second later.

This time the ground was as hard as she would have expected.

There was a distant survival instinct urging her to roll over onto her back swinging and kicking to keep her assailant from grabbing her again, but her body, still fighting to suck in another breath of air, was slow to respond. They're going to take me too, she thought to herself. They're going to take me too and kill us both. Why won't anyone help?

The answer came to her through sound, or rather the lack of it. As she waited to be hauled off to her demise, it registered that she couldn't hear any cars, planes...not even people talking. The world was silent and dark. Her next inhale was ragged, but deep, carrying the scent of lavender on it, the thought drifted into her awareness as if through fog, first, in general form, then taking on enough specific features to inform her that she was in her bedroom. Always extra sensitive to her sense of smell and the occasional insomniac, she used lavender to help her sleep. Slowly, she propped herself up by her elbows and waited for her eyes to adjust to the little bit of light her curtains allowed into the room while closed. The gentle hum of her refrigerator started in her kitchen.

She was laying on the hardwood floor of her bedroom, beside her bed, with her duvet and some of her bed covers hanging off the side of it. Her nightstand was directly in front of her, inches away from where her head hit the floor. Her breathing had evened out, but Lindsey felt exhausted. She folded her arms beneath her into a makeshift pillow and rested her head on them just as she felt herself sink into a liquid black. As it swallowed her and consciousness drifted away, she knew with a cold certainty that what she had just experienced was far more than just a dream. It had the feel of a warning that her future and possibly her life was in a peculiar kind of jeopardy and she was running out of time to save it.

***

The screech of her alarm clock broke Lindsey's deep slumber with all the force of a hammer. Her head still hurt from falling out of her bed hours earlier and bumping it on the ground. She felt her irritation at the noise warranted a gesture with more attitude than flicking the alarm button to its off status, so she crawled over to her night stand, reached behind it, and yanked the cord out of the wall.

With more effort than she felt the task warranted, she made her way to her feet. As she did so, she put another piece of last night's puzzle together when she saw the indention her swollen knuckles left in the wall just above her bed. It must have been the headboard that she was holding onto when she thought that she had a hold of her assailant's belt. The place that was supposed to be his kidney was going to need patching.

She slowly flexed her right hand while looking it over. It was stiff and painful, but nothing felt broken.

With her alarm clock silenced, she could hear children playing in the hallway outside her apartment. When she chose this unit to move into, the super had cautioned her that there was another apartment available further away from the stairwells. "Children love to congregate around stairs," the super said, "the other apartment would be much quieter."

As Lindsey began preparing for the day by picking through her closet for something to wear to work, she considered how she didn't want quiet at the time though. She wanted the sound of life around her to help keep her company. This being her first time living by herself, she wasn't sure how lonely she might become. Not just because she wasn't sharing an apartment, but because her previous roommate was the last of her female friends to get married and Lindsey didn't even have a prospect for marriage. While Lindsey's status was on purpose, there was still this sense of being an outsider to the women who knew her best, that left her feeling intensely alone.

The dream she had the night before only magnified that feeling. There was something substantial behind it that frightened her, and though she knew she needed to talk to someone about its possible implications, she didn't know who to call.

After five minutes of scrolling up and down her contact list on her cell phone, she decided to go by seniority. She and Sylvia Marin had been friends since grammar school, so Sylvia would require the least amount of explanation before being able to offer an informed opinion about what Lindsey's dream might mean. She pressed the icon to dial Sylvia's cell.

"Hey Lindsey," Sylvia answered. "Can't talk right now, can you text me?"

"I just need to shoot something by you real quick," Lindsey lied. She was hoping if she could start her story, Sylvia might give her more time. She was also hoping Sylvia could hear the obvious distress in her voice.

The sound of something crashing in the background sounded through Lindsey's phone speaker followed by Sylvia yelling the question, "Is he bleeding?", to one of her three children. Judging by the next five words to come out Sylvia's mouth over a background wail, one of her kids had an open wound. "I'll have to call you back, Lindsey. I have the clumsiest children in the universe to attend to." Then the line went dead.

Lindsey stared off into space for the next few moments trying to quiet her mind. Her cell vibrated its indication of an incoming call and a brief moment of buoyancy lifted Lindsey who assumed that Sylvia was calling her back. That turned into the sensation of falling when she realized it was her sister, Susan.

"I'm glad I caught you! Consider this your courtesy call to confirm your attendance at your niece's birthday party tomorrow at 2 PM." There was the implication of threat in her voice warning Lindsey to choose her next words carefully.

Lindsey knew the intelligent thing to do was give her sister the 'yes' she was looking for, but she was feeling abandoned and in the midst of her sulk, she didn't want anyone thinking that she didn't have her own needs to attend to. "I'll have to run by the office first. I have a meeting on Tuesday to prepare for, and a commercial shoot happening in Portland this weekend that I'm the point person on, but I'll be there."

"On time? You knew about this party a month ago, you should be planning around it, not the other way around."

"Yes. On time."

Susan called her something outside her name and hung up before Lindsey could reply. On any other day, Lindsey would have texted a rejoinder, but she didn't have the energy at that moment. She walked into her kitchen and poured herself a cup of coffee from her automatic coffeemaker and looked over the notes she had written on the whiteboard she had installed to cover her kitchen countertop's backsplash.

On the whiteboard were sketches and mind map associations Lindsey had put together for Von Conor Clothiers, her first pitch since being put on a disciplinary watch by Rodrick Alexander. While under this watch, every account she didn't win for the next six months and any job won, but not successful, would be scrutinized and potentially job threatening.

She tried running the creative angles of what she had written on the whiteboard to see if she could glean some newfound insight while she showered and dressed for work, but she kept coming back to the sensation of nearly being abducted in her dream and the lingering sense that the dream held in it, a warning or threat.

Her phone rang again, but this time, she checked the caller ID before picking up. It was Jackie Strickland, the woman whose hard headedness resulted in Lindsey's disciplinary watch. She told the ringing phone, "You wanted to take my team to Portland instead of me taking them, Jackie. Figure it out," and rejected the call. Just in case Jackie tried to reach her at the office, Lindsey called

Razor[Gun] and told them that she was calling in sick with a migraine and that her brother was taking her to see her doctor.

She changed into clothes better suited to her new destination now that she was ditching work and with a shudder part annoyance and part fear, she grabbed her keys and headed for the door full of uneasy thoughts surrounding her dream.

Just as she was about to turn the knob to open the front door to her apartment, there was a loud bang that sounded on the other side of the door. She let out a small scream and jerked her hand away from the knob. Loud voices and screams of delight sounded from the other side of the door, mingled with the patter of several sets of footsteps running up the stairs. The super tried to warn me, Lindsey thought to herself as she stepped out of her apartment and walked down the stairs towards her apartment complex's underground garage, "but at my age, kids make noise in your life, no matter which unit you choose," she finished under her breath.

Lucien Karr
Friday, 15 December 2006

It was enough to make Lucien Karr want to choke someone out right there on the cold cement floor. He was in the midst of his most important moment so far as an artist and he was doing his best to enjoy it, but twenty out of the last thirty people to walk through the gallery doors for his first solo art exhibit only stayed long enough to suck down some of the complimentary wine and gorge themselves on the free hors d'ouvres.

Vultures, he thought to himself.

He struggled to be gracious to them as he attempted to catch and maneuver some of them back into the gallery to enjoy or at least pay some attention to his watercolor paintings, but few even begged his pardon as they departed. He felt a tug on his arm, looked to see who it was, then bent down so the gallery's co-owner, Oksana Zelenko, could whisper, "Perhaps you would enjoy this more if you concentrated on the guests who are here for the art." Lucien felt her breath heat his right ear, her mouth was so close, but her words still failed to reach him.

"I think I can turn these two," he replied and hurried away from Oksana towards a man and woman holding hands and headed for the door. "Hi, I'm Lucien, the artist on exhibit here tonight," he told them as he stopped in front of them. He positioned himself so that their clasped palms would swing into him if they kept up their forward trajectory towards the exit. Lucien's right hand extended to shake on it.

"Congratulations." The man responded, let go of the woman's hand, extended his own hand towards Lucien, but closed, to bump fists with Lucien while cutting to Lucien's right side. The woman veered to Lucien's left and they both rejoined hands behind Lucien and walked out the door without ever breaking stride. Lucien looked over to Oksana in time to see her raise her wine glass in mock toast to Lucien's success before she turned and retreated further into the gallery.

Lucien wanted to scream. Instead, he walked out of the gallery and once he hit the sidewalk, turned to the right. The first thing he saw was the backs of the couple who just disrespected him. He turned in the other direction and paced halfway up the block to calm himself. On his return to the gallery, he noticed that there were several people crowding in conversation in the space directly between the gallery's open double doors and the street. Lucien caught the eye of a tall brunette in the cluster bearing the high cheekbones that hinted at American Indian. She smiled a smile that Lucien attempted to return, but the muscles that were supposed to raise the corners of his mouth and display his perfect white teeth spasmed and projected something closer to a sneer. Her welcoming expression collapsed into one of alarm. She nervously moved her attention back towards the person in her group who was speaking, then jumped with a squeal of irritation when one of the guys in her group threw a snapper at the ground and it popped with a tiny spark next to her right foot. "What are you? Ten years old?" She complained, but only received laughter from him as an answer.

Lucien spent a moment studying the group in possession of the woman he might have slept with that night if he hadn't been so awkward with people. He could feel her peripheral vision monitoring him in between quick, uneasy glances in his direction. Some part of his mind suggested that he leave her alone, but his attention was being controlled by the part of him that was tired of being a loser. This was supposed to be his night. The first of a collection of events that would signify his arrival on the art scene in a way even his most ardent detractor couldn't argue.

Instead, he was floundering with one sale out of 16 pieces of art and only an hour left for things to become salvageable. He was further disgusted with his inability to even pull a phone number or email address on the opening night of his own solo art exhibit from a woman who had basically made the first move.

He watched until she said something to cause the two males in her group of six to turn in his direction. One of the guys threw another snapper at the ground between them and Lucien. Even though he expected the ensuing pop, he flinched. The surge of fear induced adrenaline came milliseconds before he heard the words come from behind him, "Can a girl get a hug from his righteousness?"

It took a few seconds for Lucien to process what he'd just heard and attach a name to the request, but he managed, and uttered an unenthusiastic, "Lindsey," as he turned to face her.

"Geez. Could you be any less happy to see me?" Lindsey Falco asked, but kept her arms extended in waiting for a hug. Of the 39 artist friends Lucien personally invited, Lindsey was the only one to show up. None of them, including her, had RSVP'ed and even though he could guess why Lindsey was there, he needed to hear it to soften the blow of betrayal he was feeling. He asked more tentatively than he would have preferred, "So what brings you to this neck of the woods?"

"Your show, stupid. I know it's almost over, but work's been crazy and I just got out in time to get here now," she replied and motioned her fingers to indicate that she was still waiting on her hug.

Lucien looked her up and down before deciding that she was telling the truth. He detected something else going on with her, though. They had shared an artist's work and live-in loft along with three other artists for a little over two years and even though that seemed an eternity ago, after living in close quarters with her for so long, he had a sense for her moods. He allowed her to wrap her arms around him and squeeze, before pushing her back to arm's length. "It's been what? Eight years? What are you doing now, are you still painting?" He asked, injecting as much interest as he could into his voice to make up for his lousy greeting.

"I'm a senior account manager with Razor[Gun]. We're an advertising and branding agency. Not much time for painting anymore, but every now and then, I'll wet a canvas. More importantly, why are you out here rather than in there?" She pointed at the gallery's open doors.

Some of the pain and embarrassment Lucien was suffering showed on his face. "Senior Account Manager, huh? So you've risen to the high ranks."
A trace of something flashed across her face, but disappeared before Lucien could interpret what it meant, then Lindsey replied while doing a little dance, "Your girl's got skills, and so do you, so...again, why are we out here," Lindsey's dance ended with both hands pointing at the gallery door, "and not in there?"

Lucien looked around and mentally measured the distance to the nearest group of conversationalists. He leaned in so only she could hear. "I've only sold one of my paintings."

She gave him a look that wasn't entirely sympathetic. "Toughen up," she advised and planted a playful fist into his chest. "You have your own solo exhibit. Excuse my insistence that you not wear a skirt and sensible shoes in my presence. Now, enjoy your success and let's see what you've got cookin' in here."

As she moved towards the gallery entrance, he stayed where he was. "I'll be in. Go ahead and browse. Maksym and Oksana are in there. They'll both be glad to see you."

He watched her enter the gallery and was pleased

that she made her way over to a painting, not to where
the food was. Needing to know if she was just trying to
be polite, he waited until she approached a second and
then a third painting of his before accepting that she was
there in genuine support of his work. It was in that
moment that Lucien knew that their relationship was real,
not just imagined in his head.

He turned away from the gallery and looked up
and down the street. There were still a couple clusters
of people on the sidewalk outside the gallery, but the
Indian girl and her friends had disappeared. He was
relieved. It was bad enough not selling many paintings,
but it would've been worse if he had been beaten up in
front of his own opening as well. Lindsey had inadver-
tently saved him.

He turned to see what painting she was looking
at, but she wasn't in the front room anymore. She had
gone deeper into the exhibit space. There were three
rooms total, showing off the last six months of his work
and he wished that he had learned how to enjoy these
moments better.

Looking through the floor to ceiling windows sep-
arating the gallery from the sidewalk, he counted two
people looking at his art. The other 14 he counted in the
room were clustered in groups and conversation. He felt
he might as well have not created anything at all.

He heard knocking on the window and turned to
see a guy in his early 20's wearing a striped collared shirt,
vest and jeans with a pageboy hat waving a 'come here'

to someone in the gallery. There was another guy standing next to him looking out at the passing traffic. A few seconds later, a couple of pretty girls of the same age came out of the gallery. One of the girls, a red head, asked Pageboy if he got in touch with Peter yet as she crossed the gallery's threshold.

"Yeah," Pageboy answered. "He texted me his address, it's like five minutes from here, so come on." Pageboy started to walk down the street, confident that they'd follow.

The red head ran awkwardly in her heels to catch up to Pageboy and put her arm around his waist. He leaned down and kissed her. The other guy reminded Pageboy that the car was in the other direction, but Pageboy complained that he wasn't moving after already paying for parking. Realizing that Pageboy wasn't going to wait up for them, the guy and his girl hurried from behind to catch up. When they caught up, the guy put his hand in the girl's back pocket.

Lucien waited until they were two storefronts away before falling in behind them.

There were others on the sidewalk making their way to various destinations, but Lucien stood tall enough for the question, "Do you play professional Basketball?" to be the most popular inquiry he'd ever answered. While it made it difficult for him to blend in, it also made it easy for him to keep track of his quarry.

They had traveled just over a block with Lucien tailing them before he really became conscious of what he was doing, but the realization wasn't enough to stop him. He was angry and didn't care if he did something that he might regret later. As far as Lucien was concerned, his show had effectively ended when the gallery's power went out five minutes before the reception began. The gallery was reduced to four battery operated candles and a flash light to present Lucien's art to the 46 visitors present. 13 minutes after a majority of his most ardent fans left the gallery complaining that they couldn't actually see the art under the present conditions, the outlets began delivering juice again and only one of the six remaining patrons bought a single piece.

Since then, it seemed most of the attendees were people more interested in free food and drink than his art. They belong in a restaurant, not a gallery, he mused in frustration. The entire scenario didn't, at any point, surprise Lucien though. Looking at it from a purely factual point of view and devoid of all emotion, that was how his life went and it made him sick to his core because he didn't see how he could fix or prevent the problems he tended to face. They were too random.

When he got right down to it, he felt the universe itself conspired to destroy his efforts. So, he resolved he would ride out his descent into irrelevance and obscurity doing stupid things like following twenty something's and see what the cool people did with their time. That sounded like a loser move and that was exactly what he knew himself to be at that moment.

"Do you think he'll be mad that we aren't bringing

a birthday gift?" Back Pocket's girlfriend asked Pageboy. Lucien had gone so deep into his thoughts, he unwittingly found himself only a few feet behind the couples and could now hear their conversation above the downtown LA traffic.

"He'll understand. Besides, his dad is loaded, what do you think we could've got him that he doesn't already have?"

"I guess you're right," she admitted, but in no way did she sound dejected and it was in that observation that Lucien began to understand his underlying compulsion to push himself into these people's lives. They were unflustered by the events of their day, whereas Lucien lived in a state of anxiety. It shrank and grew depending on circumstances, but it was a constant companion all the same, and well-meaning attempts to get him to lighten up, normally turned into heightened bouts of nervousness.

They turned a corner and Lucien hesitated, then walked to the post to press the crosswalk button. Once the light turned green, he figured he'd follow them from across the street. As he waited, they walked a couple store fronts away, checked for traffic and jay-walked to the side of the street he intended to cross over to anyhow. Midway down the block, they walked up a carpet that extended from the street to the front door of a high rise for residences with a fancy backlit sign designating it The Locrian. Pageboy held the door open as his friends passed inside.

Lucien's confidence in what he was doing was beginning to wane now. What was he going to do? Crash a birthday party with no gift to aid in the illusion that he belonged there?

A cab stopped in front of the building and its three occupants stumbled into the building, obviously already drunk. The thump of bass heavy music pulsed subtly in the cool air. On the top floor of the building, he could peek up at a party. There was a strobe punching light in one room, filling the window frame with brief flashes of silhouette, but the other windows were lit up and he spied on a few conversationalists reminding him of his doomed exhibit. His cell phone rang in his pocket and out of habit, he pulled it out and answered it without looking to see who was calling.

"Where are you? You're supposed to be here showing me which of your paintings belongs on the wall of my apartment. I'm not here window shopping."

Lindsey hadn't changed a bit, Lucien thought to himself. "I'll make it up to you," he said. "There's something I have to do."

"And it has to be done now?" She sounded motherly to Lucien when she took that tone with her voice.

"Sometimes the piece that completes your puzzle doesn't present itself at convenient times," he told her.

"You're an idiot, but good luck with your puzzle anyhow. We should talk soon and catch up in earnest, not like what we did tonight." Then, she hung up. If it had been anyone else, the lack of a goodbye would have bothered him, but he knew Lindsey was just respecting his wishes and getting out of his way. If only more people were like that, he thought considering his relationship with his dad.

But he didn't want to think about his family now. He was trying to work up the courage to walk into the party on the top floor as if he belonged there and see if he could pick up some of the mannerisms of the esteemed by observing them in their natural habitat, and if he let memories of his family claw their way to the surface, they would only pull him down into the very hole he stuffed them into to get away from them. Then, it would be back to breathing in soil and dung until his lungs were packed too tight for a single molecule of oxygen to find its way in.

He looked up at the stoplight on the corner of the side of the street he had to cross to get to Peter's and made a silent pact that he would go once the red hand turned into a white symbol for 'cross now'.

When the light changed, he had one foot off the curb already, the proverbial first step down a path with only his gut instinct as guide. He marched, head down and determined across the street, up the block and into The Locrian. Once through the front door, Lucien's gaze drifted upwards outside of his will, following framed oils on canvas that were easily ten feet wide by twenty feet high depicting 18th century musicians playing unusual instruments until his eyes landed on the glass and jewel encrusted chandelier hanging from a ceiling 30 feet above his head. Unable to look away, he stepped into the foyer under lost breath and what was fast becoming lost nerve, as he realized that he was far out of his league with these people.

"May I help you?"

Lucien, so enthralled by the room he'd just entered, almost didn't see the elderly Black doorman seated at a lectern off to his left, and nearly jumped in surprise by the man's voice.

Lucien took a moment, then attempted to buy himself some time to think with, "I'm sorry, I didn't catch that."

While the man repeated his question, Lucien approached the lectern and concentrated on not withering beneath the doorman's gaze as he measured Lucien with the type of scrutiny that immediately identified those that belonged in the building and those that didn't.

Lucien silently weighed the options of what answer would be best, and was close to saying that he was lost and then asking for directions to a local pizza joint he knew to be close by, but his mouth had disconnected from his brain and instead uttered, "I'm here for Peter's par...", his last syllable died as his left foot tripped over his right. He fell onto the wooden floor with an accompanying grunt.

Lying there, he could feel his face flush red and the lengthy tangle of his limbs pulse with a dull ache in the parts that came into the most violent contact with the ground. He pushed himself slowly, onto his hands and knees, bracing for the inevitable tossing he was about to receive, hoping he could gain some equilibrium quickly after being deposited on the street, but the hand hooking onto his left bicep was clumsily leading him, instead, to a chaise longue set against one of the walls. The doorman looked to be 50 or 60 years old, but was stronger than he appeared to Lucien.

"Easy there." The doorman said as he helped Lucien seat himself. He waited patiently until Lucien appeared to be able to focus his vision. "You gonna be all right?"

Lucien nodded his head in the affirmative. "Lost my footing," he told the doorman.

"Aren't you getting on in age a bit, for Peter's party?"

"No. I'm just aging poorly," Lucien answered. The doubt clouding the doorman's expression told Lucien how well his lie was received. He felt a drop of sweat run down his back.

In an effort to muscle the silence out of the room, Lucien told the doorman, "Peter makes fun of the way I look all the time, it's all good." He could hear the tremor in his own voice destroying any hope of the doorman believing him.

"All good, huh?" The doorman parroted, shaking his head. "Look. I've let a fire marshall's heart attack worth of kids upstairs for Peter's parties since he moved in and no offense intended, but you don't have the look of none of them. So what are you doing? Are you a reporter?" The last question was joined by a hard look Lucien dropped eye contact over.

"No."

"Well, what then?"

Before Lucien could answer, the elevator dinged an announcement that someone had just arrived on their floor and the doorman smoothly stood up to greet the tenant. The man exiting had brown hair with the first hints of silver streaking through it to suggest a progression of years his unwrinkled face denied. "Good evening, Mr. Pullman," the tenant said, smiling until he noticed Lucien on the couch. While the expression on the man's face remained the same, Lucien could sense the disappearance of all its civility as the intellect behind it, shifted from greeting to appraisal followed by smug dismissal, as if Lucien were waving a cup in the tenant's direction in hopes of raising enough money to buy more liquor to curl up with somewhere.

"Good evening to you too, Mr. Caillat," the doorman responded enthusiastically.

Mr. Caillat was walking an extremely furry white dog that barked once in Lucien's direction and attempted to go to him, but a sharp command from Caillat brought the dog back to him. Lucien continued to watch Caillat, noticing the casual way he exuded authority from the timbre in his voice, to his posture. Even in jeans and a polo shirt, it seemed obvious that this man was the alpha in his domain. Lucien's attention returned to the doorman once Caillat had left the building and he realized that the entire time the doorman was watching him.

"If you think they can't see you aren't one of them, you got a preacher's odds at poker for fooling anyone but yourself. You best get on. Peter and his kind prey on the likes of you. Finish the night whole."

Lucien was slow to rise. He knew there was no way he was getting past the doorman without police involvement. He nodded his assent to the doorman and made his way to the door. Before he walked out though, he turned and gave the foyer one last look over. The doorman let him, but still kept his body between Lucien and the elevator so, dejected and hanging his head, Lucien exited to the sidewalk and stopped to take a deep inhale of the crisp night air. His exhale was long and full of a failure's taint. As if his lungs sucked in hope, processed it, and emitted something foul and rotting.

There were still a few people walking the streets and a police car drove by. Lucien had begun walking back in the direction of his botched gallery reception, when someone bumped into him. The man must have been texting and not paying attention to where he was walking, Lucien thought, because he heard a cell phone skip across the ground as the person excused himself. Reflexively, Lucien looked to where the cell phone had come to rest, but it was the something next to it, that stole his attention. It was the remnant of a snapper like what the Indian girl's friend was throwing at the ground. He looked back at the door to The Locrian, then up in the general direction of Peter's party and felt a renewed sense of urgency to get up there.

The Locrian was a solitary structure with alley-ways on either side of it and Lucien walked down one of them in hopes of finding an open or unlocked entrance into the building, but the two doors he discovered were both locked. It wasn't until he turned down the alley that ran behind The Locrian, that he found a potential entry point.

The fire escape ran up to the roof, by the looks of it, and for the first time Lucien could remember, he was thankful for being seven feet tall. Using his length, he was able to reach and pull down the ladder hanging vertically from the second floor fire escape landing, but he didn't have the arm strength to pull himself up the first several rungs before gaining a foothold, so he pushed over a dumpster from a nearby alcove until it was under the ladder and climbed on top of that first to give him a boost.

Seven and a half floors up and several minutes later, Lucien paused on the fire escape stairs between Peter's floor and the one beneath, to catch his breath and wipe a thin sheen of sweat from his face. He didn't expect his heart to stop racing though, being this close to his first high society gate crash.

He took a moment to place the relationship of the spent popper on the ground to the front door of The Locrian. It was a long shot, the girl being at that party, but his gut feeling was that getting into that party was something he had to do.

Heavy drums and punchy synth sounds sprang from Peter's apartment in spite of the closed windows. From his vantage point, he could see the window leading from the fire escape into Peter's apartment was uncovered, so he wouldn't be able to linger outside it long once he finished his climb. Part of Lucien hoped the window was locked. Then he'd have an excuse for his inability to see this unsettling ambition through. He took a deep inhale, began counting and on the number five, he took the remaining steps up to the landing outside Peter's apartment and reached for the window without looking to see if anyone in the room beyond was paying attention. To his simultaneous joy and dismay, it slid up and open easily under his tug.

Aristotle Troublefield
Friday, 15 December 2006

An obscene amount of daylight stabbed into Troy Griffin's neighborhood bar as Cyrus Troublefield held the door open for Aristotle, his eleven year old son, to enter. After walking a few steps in, the boy turned solemnly to his father and waited for an indication of where his dad wanted him to sit. After the door closed, Cyrus stood just inside the doorway while his eyes adjusted to the dimly lit room before motioning to a table near the bar counter where he took a stool for himself.

Aristotle took in the other bar customers from where he sat. There were two young men in polyester suits in a booth against the far wall and a couple of old men sharing a table not too far from Aristotle's own. Only his dad took residence at the bar itself and judging by the sour look Troy wore since they entered his establishment, he knew it was a personal challenge his dad was issuing to the man.

Aristotle had been brought by the bar once before by his dad and the both had been kicked out with shouts, a threat to call the Police and a shotgun aimed at their midsections. A customer observing this had warned Troy that the buckshot would, "catch the kid too, at that range", but before Troy took his chances, Cyrus led Aristotle out of the bar while a song from Rufus played on in the background. In Aristotle's mind, the sound of Chaka Khan's voice demanding to be told something good would ever more be associated with looking headlong down the barrel of that gun for a full verse's worth of standoff between his dad and Troy.

Once outside, Aristotle was put in the front passenger seat of his dad's Mercury Capri, then watched through the passenger window as his dad pulled a buck knife out from under the driver's seat, walked over to a pale blue 1963 Ford Galaxie 500 Convertible and put it on four flat tires.

"I know it was you," he heard Troy tell Cyrus, bringing him back to the present. Aristotle looked up to see the man making angry eye contact with his dad and mopping the bar top between them with a damp, white towel.

Cyrus' answer progressively hardened with each syllable out of his full lipped mouth, "Then know next time, even a finger points at me pretending to be a gun, won't be no rubber takin' steel. I'll be slicing skin."

Troy's face lost a bit of its color. "What're you having?"

"Make Jack and Coke friendly for me." Aristotle saw a motion of his dad's hand wave above a shoulder in his general direction. "The boy can have a Sarsaparilla."

The bar door opened again and Aristotle had a brief flash of panic run through him as the thought that it might be the Police entered his mind. From the last time he was brought here, he knew he wasn't supposed to be inside that building, but the purple spot left on his arm from where his dad grabbed him, silenced his objections.

All the same, he could see himself going to jail and being only 70 pounds, winding up like their neighbor Louis, who everyone called 'Cookie' after he got out of prison on account that all the inmates had a taste of him while he was inside.

Instead of a law officer, the silhouette staining the daylight dark in the open doorway, resolved into a middle-aged, pot bellied man with a ring of curly gray hair circling from above one ear, around the back of his head and finishing above the other ear. The wrinkled forehead smoothed at the area where his hairline must have started when he was younger. The bass in his voice resonated throughout the room,

"Troy. My man." Then, sounding a little sad when he caught sight of Cyrus and Aristotle, "Cyrus T. Field and company. I heard about Momma Ro. Sorry I couldn't make it to the service today." Then he put a hand to his coveralls to push the logo for the plumbing company stitched to it out in Cyrus' direction as silent accusation of who kept him away from Cyrus' mom's funeral.

"I knew you was there in spirit, Keith," Cyrus said and raised his drink back up for a long swallow, leaving only ice left in the glass when it returned to the bar.

"Troy!" He called loudly without taking his attention off his friend and directed an angry finger at his empty glass.

Aristotle pulled school books out of his backpack and stacked them on the table except his math book, which he opened. He pulled a clean sheet of lined paper out of a folder and started his homework. It was hard to concentrate though. Memories of his dead grandmother and how much she meant to him kept pushing their way into his thoughts, but he knew he would take a couple of punches from his dad if he cried in front of him.

He looked around the bar again. The other patrons were throwing hate filled glances in his and his dad's direction, but no one was talking about them loud enough for Cyrus to take notice.

He was four refills of his root beer into the two hours his dad and Keith had been reminiscing about his grandmother when the pressure in Aristotle's bladder couldn't be ignored any more. He pushed his science book across the table and stretched in an effort to conceal his attempt to spot where the restroom was. He spotted a sign pointing to an alcove. He couldn't see the bathroom door from where he was seated.

"Dad?" Aristotle tried to put just enough voice in the room to travel to his dad's ears alone. "I need to go to the bathroom."

Cyrus turned to him with furrowed brows and irritation radiating from his voice, "Then see to your comfort." Cyrus turned to Keith. "Boy's got more problems than a math book."

Standing up, Aristotle gave up the hope that his dad would walk him to the restroom. He kept his head down to avoid eye contact with anyone as he made his way through the empty tables.

Once he got to the restroom, he realized that the restroom door swung on a hinge and had no latch or knob. He went in and midway through doing his business at the urinal, he heard the squeak of the door opening behind him and footsteps approaching. He turned to see who it was and saw one of the polyester suit guys ambling toward him. he quickly returned his gaze to the porcelain in front of him hoping the momentary eye contact didn't antagonize the man.

"You don't belong here, boy." The man told him. "This is a place for grown folks." The tap of dress shoes against tile warned of Polyester's approach. He stopped where he could stand over Aristotle while Aristotle continued to pee.

"Yes, sir." Aristotle told him, keeping his face forward. "I'm almost done."

"Are you now?" The man said. Aristotle heard the sound of a belt buckle loosened from it's clasp and ringing free, then the swoosh of leather slipping through belt loops as it was removed from the man's waist.

Aristotle tensed, the whole while, trying to mentally will the urine out of his bladder faster. The bathroom door opened again, but he was afraid to turn back and look to see who it was.

"You don't want to do that, son," he heard Keith say.

"You ain't nobody to tell me what to do," Polyester answered.

Aristotle had finished and zipped his jeans back up. He turned and backed away from Polyester, trying to get from out of reach of the belt Polyester was looking to hit him with.

"That may be," Keith said, "but the .22 aimed at your back is saying something different."

Polyester turned to find the gun aimed at him. He dropped the belt to the ground and slowly raised his hands. He turned back to Aristotle so Keith couldn't see his face and silently mouthed a threat to Aristotle's life. Aristotle kept a brave face, but shuddered inside. He never forgot the naked hatred Polyester looked at him with that day, but also hadn't seen its duplicate until he began attending the social functions his girlfriend Sandy Riseborough's friends would throw.

"We won't stay long. We're so late, the party's almost over anyways." Sandy promised Aristotle as they rode the elevator up to Peter Berendt's loft apartment. "I love you." She said, rising up on tiptoes for a kiss.

Aristotle humored her with a peck to the lips and a solemn, "Love you, back." He had psyched himself up for the world of hate he was about to enter and had no intention of putting aside his game face until her car service came to pick them up to leave later that night.

The elevator doors opened directly into Peter's living space, but there was no one there to greet them. "Peter's probably opening presents already." She said absently, leading them through the foyer.

There were heads of different game animals mounted on the walls and a chandelier made from antlers hanging in the great room where Peter was receiving his gifts. From his perch atop a bar stool, he waved a greeting to Sandy and ignored Aristotle altogether. She waved back and continued to make a way for them until she was standing next to her friend Helena Parker-Smith. Of all the people Sandy hung out with Helena was one of a select few who treated Aristotle well, so he made sure to offer her a smile as he took a place next to her and Sandy.

"What's he gotten so far?" Sandy asked.

"A couple rare rifles for hunting big game, a brand new Shelby GT and a bunch of expensive things he won't appreciate." Helena answered.

While Sandy and Helena chatted, Aristotle thought of the Sammy Davis Jr. quote about how being a star allowed him to be insulted in places the average Negro could never hope to go and be insulted. He scanned the White faces in the room and acknowledged that the only other Black person in the building besides himself, had to push the elevator button for them to enter Peter's apartment.

He and Sandy met eyes and he winked. She winked back. He had met her backstage after finishing his live set opening for Anger Damagement at Heisler Arena. He was touring with them to support his debut album, *The Recovered Odyssey of the Wayward Child*, and she was backstage courtesy of her friend, Gaelle Miranda Hirsch, who was the daughter of Marston Montgomery Hirsch, the founder of Halon Media Group, a multinational media conglomerate and parent company to Dawn Mega Records, the record label Aristotle was signed to.

The connection between Aristotle and Sandy had been instantaneous and they spent the rest of the night getting to know each other, at least that's what they thought at the time. A few weeks into their dating, she admitted that she came from wealth, but had been hiding that fact from him and he confessed that prior to signing his record deal, he had alternated between living with friends, girlfriends and couch surfing in between short bursts of homelessness because he had been kicked out of his parent's house at the age of 16. When she pressed why they would do such a thing to their only child, he became defensive and refused to talk about it. "It's too depressing, and anyways, now I can make my own way in the world with this deal." He told her. "The past needs to stay behind me."

"How did you graduate from high school?" She asked.

"I didn't." He admitted and he watched as the disappointment rose across her expression. "How could I?" He demanded. "I was too busy finding something to eat and someplace to stay for the night." Then, he thought for a second and added, "I'm not stupid, you have to be smart to survive what I survived, so don't think I'm some inferior brand of person just because I didn't finish high school."

It took some time, but they made a peace between them that night on the subject and ever since, seemed to only grow closer, but Aristotle wondered if they could ever grow close enough that her friend's opinion of him wouldn't remain a constant threat to their happiness.

***

"Aaaannd now a two part present from your favorite wingmen on the planet."

Aristotle recognized the voice without needing to turn in the direction of the speaker. It belonged to the same jerk that threatened him to leave Sandy alone, Blain Richelieu. His buddy, Stark DuBrow was making an annoying trumpeting sound with a kazoo as he wheeled out an oversized person clearly drugged and barely conscious sitting naked in a wheelchair with small white down feathers stuck over his entire body face to foot. Only the hair on top of his head was unfeathered.

There was an audible gasp from some of the guests, including Sandy and Helena, but others clapped and cheered. A few pulled out cell phones and cameras to take pictures. Sandy and Helena began having a heated exchange of whispers.

"Pine tarred and feathered for your pleasure, sir." Blain announced as Stark pushed the guy around the room so everyone present could get a good look at him.

Peter got off of his stool laughing and circled the wheelchair when Stark stopped in front of him. "Is that the guy who came through the window?"

"I told you I'd take care of it." Blain answered.

Peter stopped and looked with expectation to Blain. "You said two parts."

"Jared! Seth!" Blain called.

Jared brought out a white bed linen. Seth, who was at Blain's side, grabbed an end of it from Jared and stepped away from him so the image drawn on it was visible. On it, was an illustration of a Lockheed P-38 Lightning aircraft drawn using a fat permanent ink pen.

"The guy drew this for you after we told him it was your birthday. What a sucker." Jared said.

"Nice!" Peter said with pride at his new acquisition. "Who is he?" Peter asked, bending down to better see the signature. "His driver's license says Lucien Karr," Blain answered.

"Well, Lucien better get famous." Peter remarked. "Any other presents?" Peter asked the twenty or so guests, leaning on the handle of Lucien's wheelchair. "What about you, Sandy?"

Aristotle turned to her like the rest of the room, but her expression was a knot of silent anger. Before anyone could ask what was bothering her, she gripped Aristotle's arm and dragged him back to the elevator.

As they were on their way, he heard Helena make an excuse for Sandy that no one would believe, but also wouldn't question.

As the elevator brought them down to the ground floor, Aristotle asked her a few times what was wrong. He figured that it had something to do with Lucien, but he wanted to know what her problem was specifically before jumping to conclusions. She pushed Aristotle away from her as she bent over and threw up on the floor.

Aristotle rubbed her back with one hand and pulled some of her dreadlocks back from her face with the other until she was done and asked again, "What's wrong?"

Sandy stood up straight, looked him in the eye and said, "We were late tonight because Helena warned me that something might happen to you. I stalled us to protect you from what I thought was supposed to be a somewhat embarrassing, yet harmless practical joke, but I was wrong about the harmless part. Blain's gift to Peter was supposed to be you tarred and feathered in that wheelchair."

Andros Koresh
Saturday, 16 December 2006

The most cluttered bedroom I'd ever been in belonged to a girl I once dated named Monica Ferra. There were so many clothes, papers and well, just things strewn across every horizontal surface in her room, that when I caught movement in my peripheral vision, I turned to see what had moved more out of self preservation than curiosity. That's when I realized that it was a muted television turned to a soap opera peeking from under a couple of t-shirts that had been tossed over the top of it.

Even her floor had been used as a makeshift surface, so that her hunt for a clean pair of socks consisted of picking up random socks starting with the ones closest to where she was standing and subjecting them to the sniff test.

After 15 minutes of this, we left for the amusement park with her jeans and boots hiding the fact that she never did match a clean pair together.

Sitting in Jackie's hotel room waiting for Lindsey to call and tell us what our play was going to be with Everain over speakerphone, reminded me of Monica's room because of the amazing amount of clutter she generated in the room during her single night stay. I spent five minutes watching the slow tilt of a pile of papers stacked on the room's desk as they continued to lean more and more precariously before falling on to a pair of woman's slacks on the floor that looked suspiciously like what she had worn during our flight into Portland. The papers missed my feet by a few inches.

Jackie cursed and told me to leave it even though I gave no indication that I was going to do anything but. She took her own advice and the papers stayed where they landed.

Yesterday, we had landed in Portland and checked into our hotel before Lindsey got back to us. More than once, Jackie wondered aloud if Lindsey was hunting for a different job since she was obviously intent on being fired from Razor[Gun]. I knew that wasn't the case after Jackie decided to escalate the search for Lindsey to the Razor[Gun] office and Rodrick informed her that Lindsey was out with a migraine, but was being taken to the doctor by her brother.

Lindsey didn't have a brother and she didn't suffer from migraines. That message was for me, telling me that something was really wrong with her and it had to do with a guy. It was part of a code she and I shared that allowed us to speak to one another on a frequency that tuned everyone else in the room out. My guess was that she had gone out for a hike on a nearby trail to help clear her mind after calling the crooked doctor my dad recommended to us for a note excusing her absence from work.

Lindsey never did call back yesterday, but instead sent Jackie a text while we were all eating dinner that the Everains left messages complaining that by sending

Jackie to supervise the filming, Razor[Gun] was sending a castoff to run the show in Portland and that's why they were going rogue. Lindsey said she didn't know what they were talking about, but that we could all discuss how we would handle the situation by phone at eight in the morning.

"What do they mean castoff?" Chaz asked Jackie the question on all our minds after she was done reading the text message.

Instead of answering the question, Jackie put her phone back into her purse with the kind of calm you expect just before an outburst of screams and gunfire and told us all, "I'll see you all in my room at 7:55 in the morning then," before getting up and leaving the restaurant.

Apparently, she took her rage out on what she packed for the trip because her stuff was strewn all over the room. Her suitcase was open and angled partially in and partially out of the closet, looking as if it had taken flight from the other side of the room before landing there. One of the bedside lamps was missing a shade and the other bedside lamp had a bra hanging from it. Other articles of clothing were laying on the floor, the dresser, the TV and the bed.

She was sitting on her bed, the mattress askew from the box springs, twirling a strand of brunette hair around an index finger with that same unnerving calm radiating from her. Araceli was sitting on the bed too, but out of arm's reach while keeping a conspicuous eye on Jackie. Chaz stood between her and the door and

Jeremy sat with his back against a wall fiddling with the pockets to the fishing vest he always wore on days he was shooting film.

Exactly at eight in the morning, Jackie's phone rang. She pressed two buttons and let the phone rest on the bed. "Hello, stranger. Have you fixed our problem?"

There was a pause on the other end that lasted long enough for Jackie to look at her phone to see if the call had dropped.

"No. All we can do is let them run the show their way for now," Lindsey said. "That is, unless you want to illuminate us as to what their problem with you is, Jackie?"

"I don't know. Perhaps you should ask them?"

"You know I did, just as I'm sure you deduced from my question that they told me to ask you."

"How unfortunate for inquiring minds."

"Yes. It is unfortunate. So we're back to doing as they say. Lyle will be running the shoot."

"That's crazy. I'm overruling you on this and taking control of this campaign myself."

"It's yours then," Lindsey told her.

Jackie spent a few seconds thinking, "What does Rodrick have to say about this? Get Rodrick on the phone, I need to get clearance on this from him."

"I'm here. Do as Lindsey said, please. That's our plan for this."

Jackie's neck turned red after realizing that Rodrick had secretively been on the call the entire time, listening, evaluating. "Okay then," She said, a bit shaky, in the direction of the phone, by the time she told us, "Let's saddle up troops, we have a hostile takeover to get to," she had her composure back.

"Let us know how it went once the day is done," Rodrick told her and the line clicked off.

10 minutes later, we shuffled out of her room with our plan to let the inexperienced tell the experienced how to do our jobs.

We arrived early to the site we had agreed to shoot the commercials at. It was the house of Gabe Hewlett, the owner of a Portland night spot that had the distinction of being the first legal establishment to sell Everain beers.

Lyle and Colleen Everain began their business using a recipe for a Cascadia IPA beer and a 1952 Ford F600 pickup truck to haul their homemade brew to friends and family before broadening their scope to fraternities and sororities. As word of mouth grew and new recipes were added, a promoter for underground music concert events began buying kegs of different Everain brews for their illegally held events in warehouses and other venues in danger of a police shut down.

Gabe's role in our marketing campaign storyline was him voicing over what he saw in the Everain's micro-brew concoctions that convinced him to stock their beer, champion them regionally and help put them in a position to get the business loan needed to expand and go national.

Jackie's cell rang and she had it up to her ear in

an instant.

"Is that them?" Chaz asked referring to Lyle and Colleen as the rest of us took wicker seats around a wicker table full of chips, salsa and unopened Everain beers. Jackie gave a terse nod and then whichever of Lyle or Colleen was on the phone with Jackie must have told her something she didn't want to hear, because her neck turned red and she quickly moved herself and the phone out of the covered patio and into the back yard taking her conversation well away from the Hewletts.

While she paced on the grass, making sure her lips weren't visible for any of us to read, the phone rung in the Hewlett's house and Gabe went in to answer it.

"Can you stop with the crunching?" Araceli asked us.

While she was shooting her documentary footage of Jackie pacing and trying to talk our client out of their stupidity, Chaz, Jeremy and I were eating the chips and salsa Gabe had put out for us.

"What's the difference? You can't hear her conversation anyhow," I said.

"We're still going to go back over the footage and no one wants to hear you guys biting and chewing." Araceli shot back.

"Sounds like someone could use a margarita." Chaz said.

"Chaz! A bit of trivia for you. When people were calling you a gutsy director, it wasn't because of the risks you took, it was because of that large protrusion of flesh

hanging over your belt buckle," Araceli countered.
Chaz chuckled, said. "I'm not *that* fat. Besides, I'm still
getting more action than you."

"That's nice. Your hand stopped falling asleep on
you?"

"Hey look at that funny thing on the camera that
looks like a microphone." Jeremy said right as Chaz was
about to tell Araceli something more.

"Ow!" Chaz complained, looked up, cussed and
attempted to duck under the wicker table we were all
sitting at.

"What's wrong with you?" Jeremy asked as we all
were watching Chaz hoping to figure out what he was
doing on the ground, then Jeremy too, made a complaint
and turned in the direction of the door that led into the
house, "What the..."

That's when I felt a sting in my arm. I grabbed
where it hurt with my opposite hand, expecting to swat
away the bee that stung me when Araceli yelled, "Gun!",
and ran with her camera out through the screen door
leading to the backyard.

I watched Gabe squeeze off two shots from his
pistol in Araceli's direction, but both shots missed.
"That's a BB pistol!" Jeremy yelled.

Chaz picked up his wicker chair and with a yell,
threw it at Gabe, who ducked safely, back into the
house. I grabbed two unopened bottles of beer off of the
table and waited with one raised above my head. The
moment I saw Gabe come back into the doorway, I

pitched the bottle at his head, but it broke against the wall next to him. The bottle that flew at him from Jeremy's direction hit him in the face.

"Get off my property." Gabe yelled, wide eyed and panicked through his hand while clutching his nose. "Colleen just called and the shoot is off. What are you doing here? Get out of my house!"

Chaz, Jeremy and myself grabbed our gear and all ran through the screen door into the back yard, at just about the moment Jackie was coming in to see what all the commotion was about. While still moving in the direction of the gate leading to the front yard, Chaz told Jackie, "Time to vacate, our talent is shooting the crew with a pellet gun."

Jackie glanced in the direction of the screen door, but followed after us through the side gate. Once we were in the rented minivan, we picked up Araceli who was sitting on the curb at the end of the block.

"You would have made a terrible Marine," Chaz told Araceli as she got in the car.

"You would have made a dead one," Araceli said, then to Jackie, "Now what are we doing?"

Jackie pressed on the accelerator as Araceli buckled her seatbelt. "We're going to meet these idiots and I'm either going to save this campaign or put a second bullet into its head to make sure it's dead."

"Are they going to shoot at us too?" Jeremy asked. "Not if I can help it." Jackie answered and everyone got quiet.

I sent a text to Lindsey asking what was wrong and then I sent a text to Tessa to see if she heard from Rudy yet. Tessa texted back a 'no', but also that she was working on lyrics for a new song. I texted back, 'great' because she needed the practice. She had decent song ideas, but the way she strung words together was horrid. My hope was she'd improve sooner rather than later, but like I told the guy at the hostel after he criticized her, it takes time and patience as well as a certain skill to craft words in a compelling way. I just hoped she had the work ethic to one day accomplish that.

"Leave the gear in the car, except you Araceli, I know Rodrick is going to want to see this. If things get ugly, everybody evacuate." Jackie instructed once we were at the Everain residence.

Jackie led the way to the Everain front door and knocked with authority. When Lyle opened the door, she told him, "You heard something about me that disturbed you. I understand that, but what you have standing in front of you is something a rumor can't give you...Verifiable proof that I know my job better than most of the riff raff you'll encounter. If you allow me to pitch the campaign I think you should run rather than the campaign we came up to shoot, I think you'll one day consider this decision to be one of the pivotal moments in your future growth as a company and as a national player. So, shall we get to the next chapter in your history?"

Lyle looked skeptical, but after a mumbled exchange between him and his wife, he opened the door wider in invitation.

Jackie brushed past Lyle and Colleen both, then waited just far enough inside to allow Araceli, Chaz, Jeremy and myself to come in and for Lyle to shut the door.

"Lead the way. All I need is five minutes," Jackie told Lyle.

"You aren't getting your computer, projector or anything?" Lyle asked before we went any deeper into his house.

"Do you remember how Everain Beer started?" Jackie asked.

"Of course I do," Lyle said, mildly offended at her stab at his memory.

"Then we're set."

Lyle brought us into a spacious living room and took a seat on the couch next to his wife. "You guys stand over there and keep quiet," Jackie said to us, then as she turned to face the Everains again, said, "Something was troubling you before we ever arrived. Thinking it's me is a natural impulse because I'm new to this equation, an unexpected shift from an expectation that already had you on edge. You see, if it had been Lindsey here, she'd be talking you down off of the ledge with reassurances about Razor[Gun]'s plan for your campaign, but I can't do that because I think the campaign blows."

Jackie let that last sentence sink in a few seconds. When she started back in there was force behind her voice. "You were uneasy because the campaign didn't touch upon your essence. You two built this thing with an outlaw mentality and a recipe and you sustain it in much the same way. You even drive a Ford like a couple other outlaws we know named Bonnie and Clyde. Of course you don't want to highlight that your first regular patrons were mostly under aged, but we can still keep the Everain mentality in how this nation and eventually the world gets to know you. You are outlaws and you are free from the rules that govern the weak and the unimaginative. That is what people need to know because your customers are outlaws too and if you're going to believe what you just heard about me, then you know I'm an outlaw myself and I'm willing to commit to our kind and introduce you to new outlaws with a campaign that does you the kind of justice you won't mind being handed." Jackie was in a full roar now, stalking back and forth in front of them, yelling at the Everains, "So are you in this with me, or are you going to find some accountant with some ink on his arms who thinks he knows what an outlaw is because he saw a Western when he was a child?"

She crossed her arms and waited after she finished her pitch.

Lyle and Colleen looked at each other, communicating without a sound between them until Lyle nodded, "How long do you need?" He asked.

"I'll have a treatment for you tonight and if you approve, we can begin filming tomorrow, although the bulk of this campaign should be print. This campaign calls for grassroots."

Chaz started muttering to himself as soon as Jackie mentioned having a treatment done that night.

"Sorry about Verse Eye." I told him.

"We're about nine hours away from him on stage. The dream is still alive," Chaz said.

"What do you think she did?" Jeremy asked me in a whisper so Jackie wouldn't hear.

"I have a cop friend that used to volunteer for duty on most of my shoots in Pasadena. I'll see if she has a record," Chaz offered. "In the meantime, she just took over Lindsey's account when she was the reason the account was almost lost an hour ago. Lindsey better watch her back with this one," Chaz told me.

I didn't want to, but I had to agree. I checked my phone to see if Lindsey texted me back, but she hadn't. I sent another text and gave her a brief account of what happened.

After winning back the account for Razor[Gun], Jackie brought us back to the hotel with orders to grab our laptops and other design resources and meet back in the hotel business center. We had 10 minutes to get our stuff and be there.

On the way up to my room, I took a chance and called Evan. He picked up on the third ring. Apparently, he no longer had my number programmed in his phone because I had to tell him who I was.

"Oh." Was all he had to say after I reintroduced myself.

"I'm in town. Portland, I mean, and was wondering

if you wanted to grab a beer and catch up while I'm here."

There was silence for an awkward amount of time.

"Hmmmm...yeah. I don't think that's gonna work."

"We could meet up for coffee if you like."

"What are you up here for again?" He asked. His tone of voice left me thinking that the truth would only depress him further.

"I helped move one of my cousins up here from Los Angeles, switched up driving the U-Haul and moving the stuff into the house. I'm here until Monday if tomorrow works better for you or Monday morning we can grab coffee if you like."

"Naaahhh. I think it probably best if you just delete my number out of your phone."

After hearing that, it was only with the greatest restraint, I kept myself from telling him why I was really in Portland because at that moment, I stopped feeling sorry for the guy and started thinking he deserved to waste away if this was the effort he was putting into life. We were never best friends, but we had been decent enough of friends for me to expect better than that. Even though I knew it wasn't about me, it was directed at me and that was enough.

"Consider it done." I told him, wanting to add that if he ever changed his mind to reach out, in spite of my anger.

"Thanks." He said, then was gone.

I made it back down to the hotel business center in eight minutes. Jackie, Chaz and Araceli were already there. Jeremy came in right behind me.

"Why are you all frowned up?" Jackie asked me.

"Phone call from a friend that I should have avoided."
She gave me a look that suggested that she thought I
meant Lindsey if I read the beginnings of that smirk cor-
rectly. I just let that go. This wasn't Lindsey's first loss
and if she thought Lindsey was going to hoist a white flag
over this, she was crazy.

"Now, how about we focus on the task at hand,
people." Jackie said and we were back in the business of
mapping out a campaign, but for the first time for us,
with Jackie taking the point and directing the intellectual
traffic.

Chaz' faith in our ability to knock the details out
quick was well placed. Jackie had a definite plan and
scope for the campaign that made me think that she had-
n't been winging her impromptu speech to the Everains.

I quietly wondered if she had been the source of
the leak for whatever info the Everains had been made
aware of about her.

The "tissue session" where Jackie pitched our
finalized ideas to the Everains required no tissue. Instead
of a response that induced tears and a need for tissue,
the Everains loved the concepts and expected delivery
of the printed materials within seven days.

Chaz was elated. "Verse Eye! Who's with me?"
Chaz asked, nodding his head to an imaginary beat.

I volunteered quickly, then when I realized that I
was the only one, dropped my enthusiasm. Jackie waved

us off though. "Go to your show. You all know your assignments. Just be ready to give me something by noon tomorrow. We'll meet backhere then."

Chaz said, "Okay." and headed for the door before she could recant her decision. I followed his lead, but we ended up missing The Lackwits entire set. "That's alright." Chaz said. "I'm really here for Verse Eye anyways." and once Verse Eye took the stage, I understood why.

Except for a few whistles and a few females declaring, "I love you Verse Eye", the room went quiet the moment the house lights dimmed.

The show started with a keyboardist on stage alternating between two chords. The first chord, dissonant and tense; the second chord, releasing the tension as fog machines clouded over the base of the stage. At about the time the swirling white clouds had completely covered the floor and began cascading off of the lip of the raised stage, a percussionist added an oddly syncopated rhythm to the mix and the keyboardist added a transitory chord in-between the ebb and flow of dissonance he was creating.

Two bars in, the drummer made a different kind of sense of the preceding sounds coming in on the two instead of the one or the three and before I knew it, another keyboard, a bass guitar, two rhythm guitarists and two female singers had joined the slowly building musical crescendo adding texture to the sound mass.

There was a rumble beginning to grow in the crowd and the band was matching it. Then, once the room felt like it could take no more pressure, Verse Eye took the stage and the band catapulted into a high energy funk song that was only barely audible over the screams and shouts from the audience.

He started center stage, but worked his way around it from song to song engaging with the audience members right in front of the stage, to the sides and those in the back of the room as the next song brought the energy back down a bit, the third a little more and then on the fourth song, Verse Eye pulled out a harmonica calling himself a blues harp player.

The band behind him chilled while he told a story of his blues harp hero, Sonny Terry, and how a song that Sonny performed for a Broadway show came into existence. The song would eventually come to be called *Shouting the Blues.* The start of the song had the cadence of a steam powered railway train and as he got deeper into the song, Verse Eye began throwing in whoops and hollers in between bursts of breath into and out of the harmonica. His left hand waved a dance around the instrument, muting and filtering the music in a display that went beyond breath control and extended into the physics of sound before the band joined him and they segued into a hip-hop slanted, blues inspired piece about a man who passed out drunk one night and woke up the next morning with a noose around his neck courtesy of the wife he was cheating on while he was getting drunk.

They were halfway through that song when I got the text from Tessa. "Rudy hated the demo! I'll never be a singer." It read. I immediately got my hand stamped from the dude at the door and made for the street where I could speak to Tessa without all the concert noise.

There were a lot of people milling about right in front of the club, so I made my way down the block a little where there were fewer of them and stopped.

"What's up?" I heard from behind me. It was Chaz. I kept the phone to my ear because her line was ringing at that moment. "Family drama," I replied.

He caught up to me. "Do you need me to hang around?"

"Nah. Go on back. I should be there in a minute." He gave a single head nod of acknowledgement and went back in to the show just as Tessa's line crossed over to voicemail.

"Hey Tessa, I'm sorry about Rudy. Call me back and we can talk about it. I'm disappointed too, but he's not our only avenue." It started sprinkling rain so I zipped up my hoodie and pulled the hood over my head. I made sure my ringer was up all the way and put my phone back into my front pocket.

I listened as the tires treading down the rain-slicked street suddenly became louder than the engines powering most of the vehicles. The combination of tires sounded like an impossibly large pan of grease sizzling over a stove fire. Unlike in Los Angeles, the streets didn't thin out of people so quickly once things started getting wet. I walked in little circles while I waited for the callback, eyes not seeing much that was actually around me because I was too focused on my stress.

When I returned to the show and found Chaz, he had offered to listen if I needed to talk, but I didn't want to. After the show was over, I called Tessa three more times and left three more messages before I gave up for the evening with a growing concern each time she didn't pick up. I knew how sensitive she could be from when that poet started criticizing her clichéd imagery the day we met at the open mic night at the hostel.

She had cried miserably for half an hour after I pulled her out of the room that evening and got her seated in a coffee shop up the street.

A week later, she confessed that she was glad that we talked because she had been considering suicide. Knowing that it had crossed her mind then made me wonder how she was taking this new critique from someone who was established in the industry.

I tossed and turned for an hour before sleep took me. The images I saw in my dreams didn't help settle my nerves one bit.

Lindsey Falco
Saturday, 16 December 2006

Lindsey was late. The birthday party for her niece had started two hours ago, but after her phone call with the team up in Portland, she spent a couple hours with Rodrick getting his take on the direction the political winds were blowing inside Razor[Gun]. It seemed peculiar to her that Jackie came to Razor[Gun] from Spence Wagner's shop, a place with a near zero voluntary turnover rate, put in two months in the New York Razor[Gun] office before being asked to audit one of Lindsey's accounts in just enough time to torpedo it and wind up transferring to the Santa Monica office to oversee Lindsey's progress during Lindsey's six-month probation.

Rodrick agreed that something was going on, but he wasn't sure what. At least, not yet.

"Even if we're wrong about these signs we're seeing, always be prepared to not be working here." He advised. "That's what I'm doing."

After talking to Rodrick, she swung by Lucien's place to tell him which of his paintings she bought and congratulate him on the work he did, but he answered neither his door nor his phone.

Too bad he wasn't around, she thought as she looked for parking, she could have dragged him to the party so she would have someone to talk to that wasn't going to blather about their children all day.

She paid an unannounced visit to Sylvia, but had no stomach for telling Sylvia about the dream anymore. Sylvia's son had managed to break an arm falling out of his treehouse and after three attempts to get Sylvia off that topic, Lindsey gave up and just started "Uh-huh"ing her. When it came to kids right now, she was over it already. If Susan hadn't called an hour ago and inquired with some choice threats and expletives why Lindsey wasn't already at the party, she might not have come at all.

She let out a sigh of defeat. There were so many cars along the block that she had to drive several houses up before she found a spot to park. Popular kid, she thought. I never had anything this big growing up.

Before getting out of the car, Lindsey pulled down the driver's seat vanity mirror and gave herself one last look over. She smiled into the mirror to see how it felt on her face and judge how convincing she could make it. She wasn't impressed, but decided it would have to do.

There were balloons tied to the mailbox standing by the driveway entrance to help the first timers find the house. She wondered why they were needed when there was a bouncer in the front yard full of screaming children and a couple of ladies inside it desperately trying to extract a crying child from it. While crawling and failing to keep their balance, at least a dozen children were jumping all around and sometimes into them laughing at the adults and mocking the crybaby. One of the ladies looked about ready to vomit from motion sickness.

Lindsey walked faster to the front door hoping they didn't see her and ask for her help. One of them saw her right as she got to the front door and called for her, but Lindsey was inside the house with the door shut before a second request for help could be uttered.

Inside her sister's house, she was greeted with a shock of music and celebration. She reminded herself to look happy that she was there and waded her way through the throng of partiers. There were another 15 people in Susan's living room, laughter coming from the kitchen and more people crowded outside in the back yard. Two of her nieces ran past her playing some game with their friends and shot up the stairs to the second floor. She spotted her nephew by the fireplace talking with some of his friends. He was the oldest of the four children and the only boy. She waved at him and he responded with a small raising of his head in her direction. He was already too cool to wave to his aunt.

The house was also full of the smell of grilled burgers and hot dogs. She knew that her mother wouldn't allow anyone to take over the grill while she was present, so Lindsey went straight to the backyard.

She waited until she was close enough to her mom that she didn't have to yell over all the crowd noise to ask, "Who are all these people? I thought this was for Megan?"

Her mom was obviously irritated with her, but still appeared happy to see Lindsey. The uneasy smile left her lips when she saw the left side of Lindsey's head. "Never mind that. What happened to your head? Has a doctor looked at that yet?"

Lindsey let her mom inspect it closer. As her mom turned her head to different angles to get a better view of the bump, she answered, "I fell out of bed and no, a doctor hasn't looked at it yet."

"Well someone needs to check that out before you go to sleep tonight."

"I already went to sleep with it and you don't see me leaving ectoplasm anywhere, do you?"

"Keep sassing me." Her mom encouraged waving the barbecue tongs threateningly.

"Sorry." Lindsey heard herself say insincerely. Her mother was still wearing the expression that demanded an explanation before the conversation would be allowed to change, so Lindsey volunteered, "I had a nightmare and fell out of my bed. It's no big deal."

The expression on her mother's face darkened and her eyes narrowed, she flipped a couple hamburger patties with a little extra force so they both made a smacking noise as they returned to the fire, then replied, "I told you watching those horror movies isn't good for you. Plants seeds for all kinds of evil things to grow in your mind."

Before Lindsey could respond, her sister sarcastically said from the sliding glass doorway, "Thanks for coming, Lindsey. We're overjoyed you could make it."

"I love you too, dear sister," Lindsey responded in similar fashion.

Susan's face never hinted at a smile, even as she walked over and gave Lindsey a hug.

"I'm still mad at you." Susan said. "But I'm glad you came."

Lindsey extended her arms out with her palms up in supplication and told her, "I'm sorry already."

"So what are you two talking about?" Susan asked.

"Mom is telling me about the evils of horror movies."

"Oh." Susan's frown shifted to a look of distaste. "And we move on."

"Move on nothing." Their mom told Susan. "Look at your sister's head."

Susan did and after seeing the bump asked, "How did you get that from a horror movie?"

Lindsey shrugged.

"Never mind." Their mother told them.

Lindsey and Susan smiled in triumph at each other.

"So why couldn't Andros make it to the party, again?" Susan asked Lindsey.

"He's working on the Everain Beer Microbrewery account and everyone with film experience at Razor[Gun] had to fly up to shoot the commercials up in Portland this weekend. He gave me a present to give to Megan, but I forgot it." Lindsey answered.

Susan scrutinized Lindsey silently.

"I'm not lying and covering for him, if I couldn't get out of coming to this thing, do you think I'd give him a pass?"

Susan seemed satisfied with that explanation. "So how's work otherwise?"

"I was put on probation last week and the shoot in Portland, an account I won by the way, is sounding like a disaster."

Susan's scowl returned. "Probation? For what?"

"I was over this account for Turnbull's doing a branding package for their three properties. One is a custom car interiors company, another is a high performance engine building company and the last is a custom body-work and paint company. I made my pitch, got their business, then Jackie Strickland from the New York office put in her two cents and retooled my ideas into a single brand and had me deliver that to Turnbull's. Now, Turnbull's already said that they had no intention of combining the three brands, which is why I kept them separate in my creative, but Jackie decided that was dumb business on their part and made me consolidate my work into a single campaign, which enraged the Turnbull family and cost us the account. Since, it was technically my account, it's my fault, even if it was Jackie's bad call."

Lindsey sat down on a bench near where her mother was grilling the food, "So, I still have my title and pay, but I'm being shadowed and second-guessed by the mental midget that put me in this position in the first place...Jackie."

"Joy," Susan muttered.

"That's life working for an agency," Lindsey finished, then a thought occurred to her and she reached into her purse and turned off her cell phone. Just in case, she thought to herself.

"You need to go freelance."

"Don't I know it. Where's Greg?" Lindsey asked about Susan's husband.

"Getting ice. It doesn't matter how well we plan, we always seem to underestimate our need for ice."

Lindsey had stopped paying attention to the line of people who kept coming up to her mother to grab burgers and hot dogs off the grill, so she almost jumped when she heard a familiar, but unwelcome voice announce, "I haven't seen that face for years. However are you doing, Lindsey? Hopefully better than your appearance would have us believe." It was Cassie Baumgartner, the first of her girlfriends to marry and start sprouting babies, looking as smug as ever.

"Rough night at the women's roller derby match. We won though and that's what matters," Lindsey lied.

"How quaint. I didn't know people still did that." Cassie's expression was one of derision, but Lindsey was happy to see Cassie's smile leave her face.

"Well, it isn't for everyone. I can see why you wouldn't be interested in it. You have to be pretty tough, in shape," Lindsey patted Cassie's slightly protruding belly, "and be able to take a beating as well as give one. I enjoy it though. I knocked out two teeth from one woman just last night. I still have them in my car. Want to see them?"

"No." Cassie answered before Lindsey had completely finished the question and stepped back out of

Lindsey's reach. "That's quite alright. You are right at that. Not my type of fun." Cassie giggled uncomfortably. "I prefer tea at Huntington Gardens myself or other entertainments of culture."

"Entertainments of culture? When did you start talking like that Cassie? Where's the girl I hung out with, that was dating a biker dude and planning to buy a Harley?"

Cassie looked around to make sure the wrong people hadn't heard the remark, before replying, "People grow up Lindsey. And I go by Cassandra now. Anyways, Jerry was an overgrown child, so I moved on and found a wonderful man of the world who takes great care of both me and our children. I don't expect you to understand fully at this point in your life, but I hope one day, for your sake, that you do."

The vein of jealousy running through Lindsey began to throb. "That's deep," she replied. "So, he's rich. I get that. How old is he?"

"Young enough to keep me quite pleased. Thank you very much."

"Perhaps," Susan broke in, "we should move the conversation into lighter territory. Is Nutmeg going to spend the night tonight?" Susan asked about Cassie's daughter.

"Yes, she is. I have her overnight bag in the trunk of my car. We'll take it out before we leave." She shifted her balance from her heels to her toes, then back to her heels again. It was a nervous tell, Lindsey noted that

Cassie hadn't grown out of. "If you'll excuse me ladies, I believe I could use a drink. I'll be seeing to my thirst."

As Cassie walked away, Lindsey gave Susan an incredulous look. "Nutmeg?"

"Her husband is a personal chef and also runs a catering business, so she named their kids Nutmeg, Pesto and Thyme."

"That's just evil. Are any of them boys?"

Susan smiled. "Pesto is."

"He better know how to fight."

"Come on, I could use a drink too."

Susan and Lindsey found Cassie in the kitchen with a man easily 30 years her senior wearing a fine tailored black suit and a red bow tie with white polka dots on it. They were talking to another couple, but Cassie was the first to notice Susan and Lindsey entering the room and suddenly looked uncomfortable. She turned her attention back to the couple she was conversing with and ignored Susan and Lindsey.

Susan took the initiative. "Hey everybody, this is my sister Lindsey."

Then turning to Lindsey, added while pointing to each respective individual, "This is Fred and Becca, their daughter goes to school with Megan and this is Cassandra's husband, George."

Still feeling small between their exchange outside and her being the last of the unmarrieds, Lindsey decided to get to know her husband a little better. "So you're George, Cassie was just telling me about you. She and I used to party together," Lindsey said.

George smiled at Lindsey, "Really?"

Lindsey wedged her way between George and the counter he was standing next to.

"Yep. So, if you ever need a little dirt on the old girl. Give me a holler. I've got some stories that will knock you down and halfway out."

Cassie held her fury in check, barely. She had begun to speak, but George raised a hand towards her in a gesture indicating he wanted to hear what Lindsey had to say.

"I might just play that card one day. For now anyways, my Cassandra is nothing short of an angel."

Lindsey could see a triumphant smile begin to raise on Cassie's lips without even looking directly at her. Inside, Lindsey grew a little angrier. Outwardly, she told George, "Keep it in mind. Remember, Satan was an Angel."

The smile disappeared from Cassie's face.

"You are quite the pistol, aren't you?" George asked.

"Kind of a hair trigger, some have said." Lindsey replied.

"You don't believe that what Cassandra and I have is real. What is it that you think you know that we don't?"

"Look, it's nothing personal." Lindsey answered, defensively.

Susan inserted herself in between George and Lindsey. "I need help getting some of the presents down from upstairs. Now, come be a good elf and help Santa bring them down." She told Lindsey.

"I don't know who hurt you Lindsey," George called to her back as she was being ushered out of the kitchen by her sister, "but you don't have to remain damaged. It isn't too late for you."

While steering Lindsey out of the room, Susan told her, "Don't you say a word." Then, once they were up the stairs and out of earshot, Susan asked, "What's wrong with you? Why are you acting this way?"

"It's complicated. I can't explain it in five minutes." Lindsey answered following Susan into Susan's bedroom.

"Try." Susan sat on her bed and patted the bed next to her, indicating that Lindsey should sit as well.

Lindsey sat. "Well, I haven't told anybody about this, but over the past month I've been having these dreams. Not just regular dreams, but lifelike ones where I wake up feeling like I came back from someplace that I traveled to while asleep."

"Like sleepwalking?"

"No. I mean I feel like I went someplace else for real. Like my soul or something, while my body stayed behind. I know it sounds nuts, but it's what it feels like. But, anyhow, in the dreams, I'm married and we have a daughter. The weirdest thing about them is they continue, one after the other like a soap opera."

"Okay, and what happens in these dreams?"

"They started with my daughter, Melanie, and I visiting my husband's cousin while on vacation in Niagara Falls, the Canadian side. My husband had to stay at home the last minute before we left because of something on his job, so it was just the two of us traveling. I can't recall the cousin's name, but it feels like we've been friends for years. I don't want to admit it even to myself, but I'm wondering if what I'm seeing is maybe my future. Either that or it's some kind of warning. Either way, I have a gut feeling that the outcome of these dreams are going to have consequences in my waking life."

Susan had a grave look now and nodded her head. "Are these dreams how you got that bump on your head?"

"Yes and no. In the dream our daughter was kidnapped I think and then while trying to find her, someone attacked me from behind. While I was fighting him off in the dream, I fell off my bed and hit my head on the floor."

"Wow. Come here." Susan said, gesturing with both hands for Lindsey to come to her and Susan gave her a tight hug.

Lindsey began to cry. "I don't know if I'm going crazy or if I'm somehow in real danger."

"I don't know, hon." Susan said still holding her. "I know someone that might be able to help, though. Her name is Imoleen and she's done a lot in dreams before and might be able to give you some good advice. I'll call her tomorrow morning."

"Can you do it now?"

Susan made the call and left a voicemail. "She'll get back to me. Until then, do you want to stay with us? You can take the spare room and I'll move Megan's sleepover downstairs."

Lindsey accepted the offer.

"I hate to sound callous, but we need to get back downstairs."

"I know."

After they had rejoined the party, she kept herself busy cleaning behind people and staying out of the way until the parents went home and six eight-year-old girls took over the downstairs floor for their sleepover.

As she drove home to pick up a change of clothes and personal items, she tried to analyze the facts of the dream and question the parts that seemed odd, like why wasn't her husband with her and their daughter? From what she could piece together from conversations and situations in her dreams, it was due to his job, but what was his job? Could he be the reason their daughter went missing? Why was she attacked?

A horn sounding behind her, brought Lindsey back to the present. She looked up to see that the light had turned green and pressed on the accelerator still thinking. She realized that her opportunities to find all that out was most likely behind her now that her dreams progressed beyond her hanging out with her husband's cousin and was instead in the midst of fighting off being kidnapped or worse and since she had no real prospects towards marriage, she had no inkling who her dream husband might be. A curse slipped out under her breath.

Later that night, as she laid down for the evening, she reminded herself that she needed answers if she could fight off her attacker and find a way to get some. When she fell asleep though, she had no dreams.

90

Lucien Karr
Saturday 16, December 2006

Lucien eased himself into an upright position, looked around the sunlit room, didn't recognize it, felt a wave of nausea, then laid back on the bed trying to gather his thoughts. He had the notion that he was on a bed, but it didn't sound like a regular mattress beneath him.

He kept his eyes closed because the room was too bright, then rocked slightly back and forth to recreate the noise and slowly figured out that it was the sound of thick plastic crinkling beneath him, but that didn't make sense. He moved again, more crinkling. Attempted to sit up, but slowly this time and opened his eyes. I've grown feathers, he thought and found that funny, but it hurt to laugh.

He gave his surroundings another look over and felt some comfort because he wasn't the only animal in the room. There were several others in there room with him, but something was off. He laid back down. It was difficult to think, but Lucien concentrated and finally understood that the other animals were only heads, put up on the wall like trophies. His head shot up and a wave of dark crossed over his vision, but when he could see again, he still had feathers and he was lying on plastic.

He felt a brief wave of panic mixed with confusion and let out a startled cry, then his eyes felt too heavy to keep open. He fell back into the waiting plastic and felt nothing for awhile.

The next time he woke, he was confronted with a horrible stink even before he opened his eyes. Fear shallowed his breath and his body wanted to go back to sleep even as part of his mind understood that it probably wasn't safe to do so and he shuddered from the cold of laying in a muddy puddle. He managed to prop himself onto his elbows. He was lying in a dark, thick liquid.

"Would you like some water?" Someone in the room had asked.

It was night-time now and the room was fairly dark and over furnished. A single table lamp burned a dull bulb. Eventually, he made out a woman sitting in a chair across the room. She was leaned forward, model thin and blond with pale eyes Lucien had trouble looking away from. His dad would have described her as 'stunning'. Lucien suddenly became very aware of his nakedness aside from the feathers that covered his entire body including his private parts. The smell from his incontinence only made it worse.

"Yes. Please." He told her more to get her out of the room than anything, although the suggestion reminded him that he was very thirsty as well as very tired.

She got up leisurely as if nothing was odd about the scenario, took a small bottled water off of the room's dressing table and approached Lucien. Her every step betrayed the sound of the same heavy plastic he was laying on. *Even the floor is covered with plastic?* He thought.

"Who are you? What is this?" Lucien asked.

"I'm Gaelle. As for what this is, you'll have to be more specific about which 'this' you're talking about." She took the cap off of the bottled water, handed it to him and took it back once she realized his hands were shaking too much to hold it himself. "Here." She said and held it so he could drink. "That's enough for now." She pulled the bottle away after he had gulped half of it down.

"Thanks." He said. "What day is it?"

"Saturday."

Lucien let that fact sink in for a bit, then, "What am I doing here?"

"Besides making a mess? Sleeping."

"Are you some kind of nurse?"

"No. Not even close. I like the picture you made for Peter, by the way."

He felt brief flash of gratitude at the compliment, then remembered that he was naked and laid back down covering his privates with his hands. "Why am I covered in feathers?"

"A little late for modesty, don't you think?" She said gesturing towards his cupped hands. "As for the feathers, you'll have to ask our host. I wasn't at the party last night, so I don't know."

He raised his head. "Our...host?"

"You don't think I'd live in a place furnished like this do you?" She said, looking like she had just tasted something awful and waved an arm in the direction of a moose head hanging on the wall. "Speaking of distasteful, when you can, you need to shower and clean yourself up.

The bathroom is through that door." She pointed towards one of two open doors.

"Could you help me to the bathroom?"

"No."

He recoiled a bit from how blunt and quickly her answer came and again tried to piece together what had happened the night before after he entered the window off of Peter's fire escape. "We're at Peter's." He said.

She nodded her head. "Maybe we're not the best people for you to be around." She said.

Immediately he connected her dismissal to what the doorman had told him the night before about these not being his people and a surge of adrenaline shot through him.

"Why? Because I'm not rich?"

"Easy there cowboy." She held her hands out as if to indicate that she was unarmed. "I meant because you're in a stranger's house, naked, covered in feathers and lying in your own excrement. Regardless of your financial class, that sounds like a string of poor life choices." She let out an uneasy laugh. "Of course my own life decisions haven't been so stellar lately." She looked back at him. "You seem nice and I thought you should be warned."

Just then Peter walked into the room and wrinkled his nose at the smell. "Warned about what?"

There was an edge to his voice, but Gaelle calmly answered, "Warned that I'm a bad influence and now...a pariah."

"It'll pass. How long has he been awake?" He asked Gaelle.

"A few minutes." She said.

Peter brushed her off with an air of dismissal, then told Lucien, "Hey there party animal. You drink like a Russian." He turned to Gaelle. "Or is it like the Irish?"

He stopped a few feet away from the bed. "When you lost that bet to Blain over the pool game, I didn't think for a second that you'd actually cover yourself with feathers. I know I wouldn't have done it. Call me a poor loser, I don't care." He turned back to Gaelle. "The guy from Spilt Milk is here to interview you. He signed the papers and then there's this." He held up a check and snapped it.

"Thanks." She told Peter and took the check, then to Lucien, "Keep at the art thing. I certainly wish I had." She was out of the room before Lucien could say anything in return.

Peter asked, "How you feeling bud? You still don't look so hot."

"Tired. Very, very tired. I did this to myself?" Lucien asked looking at his feather-covered body.

"You don't remember last night?"

"No. Not much, anyhow."

"Well. You had a lot to drink, then challenged Blain to a game of 8 Ball and agreed that the loser would put pine tar all over himself, roll around in the feathers and do the Chicken Dance for everybody. I don't think he meant for you to take off all your clothes though."

"I don't know how to play 8 Ball." Lucien felt confused.

"That would explain the whipping he put on you. Like I said, you'd had a lot to drink. Maybe you should hit an AA meeting if you're drinking to blackout. That can be dangerous."

Lucien took a few moments to rummage around in his head for any memories from the previous night and came across a vague recollection of a dark haired man in his early twenties shoving a glass of whisky into Lucien's hand and telling Lucien, "If you're gonna drink with the men, you gotta drink like a man." As near as he could tell, Lucien had drank about seven of those glasses worth of whisky at two fingers high of liquor in each round.

The first two rounds were friendly. Beginning with the third round, Lucien felt threatened by the person he was guessing was Blain, who kept some kind of glass or bottle in Lucien's hand until his memory went blank.

He asked a few more questions about the night before and Peter answered each without a second's pause. "I got a few things cooking right now." Peter said, finally. "I'll be back. If you can manage to get yourself up, there are towels and soap in the bathroom along with your clothes. There's also a jug with olive oil in there. You can use that to get the pine tar off of your skin without taking a layer of your epidermis off in the scrubbing. Use the trash bag for the feathers, I don't want my drain clogged all up. Don't leave this room before you get clean though. I've already had someone clean all the feathers up everywhere in my apartment but in here, so I'll know if you do."

Lucien took in the veiled threat in his tone. "Sorry about the mess. I didn't mean to be a bother."

"No need to apologize." Peter told him halfway out the door. "You're my guest."

"Thanks." Lucien managed, but the word wasn't filled with any gratitude, just like Peter's use of the word guest held no hospitality. After Peter walked out, Lucien made an attempt to get to the restroom to clean up before Gaelle came back in, but the effort only made him more fatigued.

Peter had closed the door behind himself and Lucien struggled to remember if there was any noise indicating he was locked in the room. He sat up and tried to focus on the knob, but he couldn't tell in the dim light whether the locking mechanism was on his side of the door or not.

His last thought before losing consciousness again was about Mr. Pullman encouraging him to leave so he could 'finish the night whole'. Lucien wondered how much of himself would be left if he ever got to leave Peter's apartment.

Aristotle Troublefield
Saturday, 16 December 2006

It had been a two and a half hour journey by bus from the room Aristotle rented from his friend and music producer, Epistrophy, to the Beverly Hills restaurant where he was supposed to sit face to face with Gloon, the new producer his record label Dawn Mega Records was teaming him up with and pretend to be happy with their choice. Aristotle had heard some of the producer's work and didn't see how they fit together, but then during the conversation where the label gave him the ultimatum of having Gloon produce his next record or be dropped from the label, the word 'sales' came up 13 times. The word art? None.

The entire way there, Aristotle fought to control his temper, but it wasn't just his situation with his label anger-ing him, he was also replaying what Sandy had told him the night before about Blain's plan to pretend to make amends with Aristotle and offer to let bygones be bygones so that he could liquor Aristotle up, slip him the date rape drug rohypnol, then strip, tar and feather Aristotle as a birthday present to Peter.

"If you knew they were trying to victimize me, why take me there in the first place?" He demanded to know as soon as they reached the street in front of Peter's building the night before.

"I just knew they had something planned. They've

never done anything as bad as that with me around. I didn't know they were capable of that level of cruelty." Sandy answered. "Helena told me what they were up to after we got there and they brought that poor man out for display. Even she didn't think they had it in them to do what they did."

"So, I'm supposed to hang out with your friends like I wasn't the intended victim?"

"They aren't my friends. Not after this."

Part of Aristotle wanted to hold her at least partly responsible though. It was her friends who did this at a party she brought him to. "I'll find my own way home." He told her. "I'll call you when I'm ready to talk to you again." The sound of her crying as he stalked off from her to find a bus stop gave him a mix of satisfaction and discomfort that he never experienced before. He wanted her to feel bad for what she almost subjected him to, but at the same time he hated seeing her in any kind of pain. Given everything that he had to figure out about what he had just heard, he figured distance to be the safest decision he could make regarding her. In his current state of mind, he was more liable to say or do something that he would later regret than he was comfortable tempting.

He had half expected her to call him in spite of his wanting space and time to think and was glad that she hadn't. It would be easier to make sense of things without her hovering around trying to explain away the situation.

It was a relief, walking into the restaurant and having his focus taken off the previous night even though the music portion of his life was beginning to suck as well.

As the host walked him to his table, Aristotle recognized a movie star dining with a beautiful woman. The movie star was twice her age plus a couple years, but both looked happy with one another's company. Each one running their game, Aristotle mused, exchanging their goods in a currency only the shallow could find satisfaction in.

Gloon had arrived early and was already seated at their table and looking over the menu. He was a large, dark man with an Afro increasing the size of his head by a factor of three. He easily tipped 250 pounds on the scale, but rose easily to greet

Aristotle. "What's good? They call me Gloon," he said.

"Aristotle..."

"Yeah, Troublefield," Gloon finished for him. "I know."

As they sat, Gloon motioned for the host's attention. "Can you send our waiter over, please." Then slang returned to his speech as they took their seats to ask Aristotle how he came up with his name.

"It's what they gave me at birth," Aristotle answered.

"That's crazy. Your parents philosophers or something?"

"No. Before they kicked me out of the house, my pops was a construction worker, my moms was stay at home."

"What they kick you out for? Drugs."

"They just didn't want a kid."

"That's rough. We can use that, though. For your tracks. Put the real out there, because what you spit on your first release was kind of everywhere and you can't have people be like, 'who is this Negro?', and expect to get followers."

Aristotle paused to think about what Gloon was saying. After he signed to Dawn Mega Records, it was his stories about overcoming the random acts of hard luck life sometimes throws at a person that had driven the tracks on his debut CD, now he was being paired with Gloon and he didn't understand why they made that choice. "Aren't you known for gangsta rap productions?"

"Yeah, but not studio gangstas." Gloon said with pride. "My heat's made with real fire. So, no I'm not here to make you sound gangsta, but to tell your story and to make you some hits. You need guidance, not just tracks. I'm here to kinda mentor you while we work together."

The waiter had returned to the table while Gloon was talking and waited patiently for Gloon to finish before speaking. "What's your pleasure, gentlemen?" He asked.

Gloon went first, saying, "Might I have your Sweet Corn Soup to start, your True Japanese 100% Wagyu Beef Prime Rib, rare, with horseradish on the side, accompanied by your Pumpkin Sage Butter Tortellini with fresh parmigiana. We'll also take a bottle of that 1999 Shiraz from the Barossa Valley that your sommelier recommended earlier for the table. Thank you." Then he gestured for Aristotle's turn to order.

Aristotle sat staring stupidly at Gloon until the waiter politely turned Aristotle's attention to what food he wanted to order. Aristotle managed to order a well done petit cut filet mignon. After the waiter left, Aristotle asked, "What's with the verbal costume change every time you talk to the staff here?"

"You really are going to turn into a project after all." Gloon said.

Aristotle didn't like how that sounded at all, but tried to hide his irritation at the remark.

"You speak to people using their native tongue when possible." Gloon said, but Aristotle still looked confused, so he added, "Take a look around you. How many Folks you see up in here?" The blank look stayed on Aristotle's face, so Gloon clarified. "Black people."

Aristotle took in their surroundings. "None."

"That makes us ambassadors of a sort. We're their window to Black people without the bias of how we're portrayed in the media."

"Okay. So why talk slang to me now, when people biased by the media are sitting at tables all around us?"

Gloon sat back in his seat with a look Aristotle couldn't read. "I'm gonna like working with you. You think about things, question them. We're gonna use that for your record and you're gonna hate me sometimes for it."

Aristotle leaned forward in his seat. "Did you sign for this gig the way I signed for my contract?" He asked, knowing Gloon would understand what he meant.

Dawn Mega, the woman who founded and gave Dawn Mega Records her name was extremely vocal about starting off as a stripper and turning down all the offers to become a video vixen until she saved enough money to fund the recording of her debut rap record *On the Eve of Mega*, which won her a distribution deal from Corn Whisky 'Cordings out of Louisville, Kentucky, thus beginning a seven year, five-time triple-platinum record selling spree that she converted into a CEO job at You Child Recordings out of Philadelphia, Pennsylvania before starting Dawn Mega Records.

Unlike many of her contemporaries though, her label wasn't a subsidiary to a larger record label, she struck a deal where Dawn Mega Records became part major record label and part music division for the multi-national media corporation Halon Media Group based out of Burbank, California.

She had done it all by the age of 29, garnering as much animosity as she did praise, but it was a quote from an awards ceremony red carpet interview that Aristotle was referencing where she famously said, "Growing in this industry, I not only found men had a taste for me sexually in a manner that helped my career, but I realized I had a taste for men sexually in a manner that helps their careers as well, and don't we all use whatever leverage we have to fulfill our desires?", when a reporter questioned her about using her position as head of Dawn Mega Records to have sex with most of the male artists she had signed.

***

"No." Gloon said. "I'm not under that kind of contract. She hired me based on my track record. I'm here because she doesn't trust your guy Epistrophy after the beats he made and the production job he did on your last CD. Personally, I hear potential there, so I'm not ready to just dump him, but I'll be executive producing whatever tracks he contributes along with the beats I supply you, giving the final yea or nay on all tracks, so let him know he's gotta come stronger than before if he wants a slot."

Aristotle was back to being irritated with the circumstances of his next record, but he already voiced his misgivings to Dawn when she insisted that he meet with Gloon and she wasn't going to budge. He had to get better sales this time around and she felt Gloon was the guy to get him there.

They spent another hour past finishing their dinner going over each other's expectations and vision for Aristotle's sophomore effort. When the check came, Aristotle was forced to use his credit card to pay when Gloon threatened that he was already doing him a favor by working on his next CD. As they parted, Gloon gave Aristotle a piece of paper with their studio schedule for the next month on it.

"You'll notice that we start Monday at eight in the morning. Blasphemous time for creating music, I know, but if you arrive at eight, that's 15 minutes late in Gloon-time." Gloon warned, then he tipped the valet driver, pulled himself into his matte black Chevy Tahoe and drove off.

Aristotle walked just over a half mile to the bus stop he needed to get himself from Beverly Hills to Epistrophy's house with minimal transfers, all the while thinking about what he was going to tell his friend, landlord and ex-producer.

In spite of the mediocre sales, Aristotle was proud of the work he and Epistrophy had put out. Aristotle wanted each song to tell a story of heartbreak and in some cases of perseverance as well. To him, that was what life was - getting back up and living like you're more than the assembly of overused, under appreciated parts we can so easily feel like and he loved the soundtrack Epistrophy composed for him.

Apparently, they were out of touch with the larger part of the buying public. They thought they had a good crossover mix between, rap and rock with progressive hints at pop, but after seeing the post tour sales figures, Dawn said his record's numbers were the stripper equivalent of being tipped in coins. "Coins hurled with force." She added as emphasis.

Now, he was going to be working with a gangsta rap producer after making a name for himself as a suburban storyteller. He had complained to Sandy hoping for a sympathetic ear and perhaps some leverage since she was friends with Gaelle Miranda Hirsch, the daughter of Halon Media Group's founder, Marston Montgomery Hirsch.

What he got instead was encouragement to see where the pairing between a poet and an ex-con turned multi-millionaire producer might lead them both. "My dad didn't raise a princess, Aristotle," She told him, "he raised me to be an adventurer. So my advice will always be to go forth."

"What am I supposed to tell Epistrophy?" Aristotle complained.

"That you're getting a second chance with some-one skilled at success. If you think this is hard, get dropped from your label."

Aristotle let that last remark close the conversation. There was no sympathy there for him or Epistrophy. Much the way he had no sympathy for how bad she felt over him almost being drugged, tarred, feathered, and who knows what other personal violations they had planned.

He stopped and realized that he was so caught up with his own brush with humiliation and who knew what else, that he never thought to call the cops to come in and save the guy who was actually victimized.

He thought briefly of calling Sandy, to see if she heard what happened to him, but he still wasn't ready to talk to her. He didn't know if he ever would again.

Too late now, he rationalized. They probably left him in the gutter somewhere to sleep it off. He resolved to watch the news the next few nights to see if anyone meeting the victim's description was missing. If so, he'd step forward to the Police with what he knew. If not, he'd continue minding his own business.

Andros Koresh
Sunday, 17 December 2006

When my ringing cell phone woke me, I glanced first at the bedside clock before reaching for the phone out of habit. "It's six-thirty in the morning. Why didn't you call me back last night?" was how I wanted to greet her, but being unsure of her mental state, I settled on, "Are you alright?"

"I broke some stuff of yours last night," she explained.

I went from groggy to hyper-alert in the span of her sentence. "What are you talking about? What stuff?"

"Your computer mouse. Your acoustic guitar, some other things. It was Rudy. He was such an ass that I got real angry and started smashing things."

I sat up in bed, angrier than my voice was communicating. "That wasn't the best response you could have had. If you're going to be an artist, you're going to have to learn how to take rejection better."

"I know." Her voice was meek now.

I resisted the urge of railing on her by reminding myself to get home and survey the damage myself before assuming how bad she messed up my things. There was also the consideration that I was too far from home to prevent her from breaking more of my stuff if she got upset with me. To do that though, I had to change the subject. "What are your plans for the day?"

"I talked to my mom. She bought me a plane

ticket back to Charlamagne. I'm on the bus to the airport now."

"So you're giving up?" I wasn't sure whether to
be irritated over the waste of my time helping her
develop as an artist or relieved that she was out of
reach of my possessions.

"Yes. No. I don't know. This isn't working.
We've been working together for three months and we
don't have any kind of deal happening."

"It takes time. Certainly longer than three
months. Don't believe the TV shows that makes this
look easy, they lie for PR reasons."

"It is that easy for some people and I'm tired of
not being one of them."

"I don't know what to tell you then."

She let me hang there. In the gap I could hear a
stop announcement from the bus driver. "Me either. I
have to go now. Bye."

"Bye." I wanted to smash something too.
Instead, I got up, got dressed and headed down to the
business center to work on mockups for the Everain
Beer campaign. Now that the campaign was going to
primarily be in print, I didn't need a team to do any
work on the thing and I needed something to occupy
my mind until I could see for myself how much Tessa
had just cost me in damages to my apartment.

Unlike the hotel gym, the hotel's business center was empty at seven AM. I powered up my laptop,
plugged in a digital drawing tablet to my computer so
I could hand draw my designs on the tablet and have
them go directly into Photoshop.

In between spurts of working on the Everain
campaign, I kept returning to that last conversation

with Tessa. She was right. There were people that record deals came easy for. Sadly for her, one of those people was her brother Angel Jr. He was ten and a half months older than her, and was a rapper who went under the name Tha Yung Luvr. He had come out to Los Angeles to become a recording artist as well.

The big difference between the two was that their dad, Angel Carrillo Sr., an action movie star in the 80's, personally flew Angel Jr. out to L.A. first class to take meetings and shop around for a deal. Two days later, Angel Jr. had a contract with Dawn Mega Records thanks to a favor pulled by an uncle who worked for Dawn Mega's parent company Halon Media Corporation as an Ad Director for one of their magazines.

While her brother was enjoying his time working with his producer Mix Kimmist on his song Alonely which had been placed in the highly anticipated Thanksgiving holiday movie Depth Perception before even being recorded, Tessa was traveling by bus to California using money she saved while baby sitting over the summer.

"The only reason Angel even got into music was because of me, then he got all the support." She had complained that first day we had met. I knew what it felt like being the outcast no one believed in and identified with her plight. That was my mistake. Just because I wished someone had looked at my work ethic and invested in me, it didn't mean that everyone deserved the chance I was denied.

Of course I would have liked to have learned all this before my belongings were trashed by Tessa.

I had an hour's worth of quiet to contemplate

the errors in my judgment in between stabs at mock up designs for Everain, before Jackie poked her head through the door.

"Mind if I have a look?" She asked.

I played like I wasn't hating the world at that moment and gave her a gander at my designs.

"Not bad." She said, flipping the designs across the screen. "The second and fifth designs show the most promise." She pushed the laptop back where the screen was facing me. "How long have you been down here? Did you stay up all night?"

"No. Just getting an early start."

"How about I buy you breakfast on Razor[Gun]'s dime. The hotel cafe is open now." She offered.

I took her up on the offer and the small talk passed the time fine by my estimation and got us through a majority of the meal before Jackie said, "So, you must be an ass-man."

All I could do was look at her. I didn't know how to respond considering that she was essentially my boss.

She scooped a spoonful of oatmeal into her mouth, nodding her head in confirmation of what she just said. "Why else would you spend all your time pushing others to the front of the stage instead of reaching for it yourself? You must love the view from behind."

"You're basing this on..."

She didn't miss a beat in finishing my sentence. "...your being at Razor[Gun] for eight years and you've never sought a promotion. You help get your friend Lindsey hired and now she's your superior." She raised a finger at me to prevent me from denying it. "I asked. Then, I hear about this singer that you're working for..."

"With."

"Whatever. Same thing. You're in the background being introduced by her when no one's paying attention rather than having your name on the marquee in the first place. Oh, don't get all angry at me. I'm not criticizing, I'm just trying to comprehend what you get out of being the help rather than the star."

"I get enough recognition."

"Does she scratch your belly too, or just pat you on the head and feed you a snack when you've done good? She certainly doesn't let you sleep."

"I'm sorry, I missed the purpose of the insight you're attempting to gain."

Jackie shrugged her shoulders. "Just good ole curiosity."

"I work with what I've got."

"You get what you tolerate."

"I'm sensing advice in my near future. Okay." I grabbed the table edges dramatically to brace myself. "I'm ready. Let me have it."

"No. I'm bored now." Jackie opened her mouth in an exaggerated yawn and motioned for the waitress to come to the table. "Check please." She told her.

"Thanks for breakfast." I said, getting up furious and grabbing my laptop bag.

She laughed. "Have those mock ups for me by noon." I heard her say seconds before I exited the cafe.

I was two steps into the business center when I realized that there were two kids in there on the internet only partially paying attention to a toddler who

was working his way around the room no doubt looking for something to break.

I changed course and headed to the elevator
and by the time I reached my new destination, I had
calmed down just enough to not punch Chaz in the
face as soon as he opened his hotel room door.

"I would appreciate your not discussing our
conversations with Jackie." I told him.

He looked confused. "What did I tell her?"

"Tessa?"

"Oh. That. Sorry, man. Consider the loop
closed."

I could tell by his expression that he had no clue
how compromised his little faux pas left me feeling.
"Thanks." I said, then marched down the hall to my
room. I worked on Jackie's mockups until just before
noon and then uploaded them to the Razor[Gun] web-
site backend for her approval. It was 12:15 by the time
the upload was finished, but I was still too angry to
care.

The room phone rang and I figured it was
Jackie demanding the files, but when I picked up, it
was someone else entirely. "Let's go get us a drink."
Chaz said. "Meet me in the lobby in ten minutes."

He was waiting with a cab by the time I made it
to the lobby and shortly thereafter, we were inside a
place with an Irish name and an English decor. Like at
the airport, his first pull of his beer was one of rever-
ence.

"What's with the fervor?" I asked after he had opened
his eyes and returned to Earth.

"Wine lovers have their introductory ritual of
tasting a new bottle and I have mine, only I'm less pre-

tentious." He took another pull.

I raised my own glass and took the top three inches off of the cola inside it.

"How's your family situation?" Chaz asked.

I was hoping to avoid talking about Tessa or owning up to the lie I told last night. "Bad. I'd rather not talk about it if you don't mind."

"I'm sorry to hear that, but no...we can talk about something else. So what did Jackie say to you about Tessa?"

I wanted to say, "Just the truth." and accidentally did.

Chaz leaned in. "What do you mean by that?"

In spite of my preference to not talk about Tessa, I told him about the text last night, the call this morning, my apartment being trashed and the back-story concerning the way her family didn't support her because I thought it was relevant to her recent behavior. He listened intently, only interrupting a couple times for clarification about this or that.

"Well, I didn't know any of what you just told me, so what exactly did Jackie say that can be attributed to my remarks?"

I told him almost verbatim how the conversation took place.

He laughed. I frowned. He asked, "When you went back to designing your mockups, did anything change about them?"

"No."

"Really? No escalation of tension or aggression coming from your concepts?"

"Okay. Maybe a little."

"She was just manipulating you to put some

testosterone in your designs. I'd put money on it. Now, the singer, you haven't heard from her since that call, huh?"

I shook my head.

"Give it a day or two and see if she calls you back and doesn't maybe make another run at it. Don't let her stay at your place, but maybe you two can work through this."

"Even after her breaking my things?"

"Man, I had these two stars on one of the movies I directed get into it so bad that one of them stole the other's $120,000 car and smashed it into a brick building.

After the film was done, the dude that smashed the car brought the other guy in on a sweet deal to make up for what he did and they are now co-producers of a successful show on cable that finished it's second season and was just renewed for it's third. They're also scheduled to begin principle photography on a new buddy pic slash action comedy, starring the both of them in three weeks. Alliances in the entertainment industry have no rhyme and usually mock reason. If you can forgive her, this all might be water under a very successful bridge between the two of you."

I finished off my cola and ruminated about what he said. While I was doing this, his phone beeped and he read the text. "They're ready for us to shoot the promos." He typed in a return text, we both got up and he dropped some cash on the bar as he led the way out.

"We aren't taking a cab back to the hotel?" I asked once we were outside and I realized he intended on walking up the street.

"No. Jackie is going to swing by and pick us up. I texted her the address to the steak joint next door, so we'll wait out front there.

I began to have some of the same reservations that Jackie had about his drinking now that he was hiding it. The crazy thing though, was he only had a single drink and that didn't jibe with what I knew about alcoholics, so I resolved to just watch and see how things played out with him and alcohol.

Once we arrived at the Everain house to shoot the promos, there was a brief tug of war regarding who was in charge of the shoot. Jackie thought the power had reverted back to her, but the Everains clarified that notion quickly.

"We're still in charge of all the shoots." Lyle said. "We like your ideas, so we incorporated them into our vision."

While Jackie attempted to negotiate the context of the shoot with Lyle, Chaz leaned into my ear and said. "They're auteurs. I hate auteurs."

Jackie eventually lost the argument and we set up our lights and cameras to capture Lyle and Colleen making batches of their home brew in their so-called brew room. It had large picturesque windows that made for an interesting backdrop, but they didn't want to begin filming until it was raining outside. "If it isn't raining, how will people know we're in Portland?" Lyle asked.

"You tell them you're in Portland." Jackie answered. "That's how this works."

"That's how Hollywood works. You're in Portland now."

We waited two hours for the rain and had lost

most of the sun for the day. Jackie reminded the Everains that we were flying home Monday morning, but the Everains insisted that they had a vision.

Once the rain started though, the audio was unusable. There was a storage shed they kept in the backyard off of the side of the house that managed to capture the water runoff from the roof in a loud display that overpowered any and all attempts to capture audio for the narration the Everains insisted should be captured only while filming their brewing process.

By the time the rain stopped, we had to change the camera angles that the Everains wanted because there were large windows in frame without any kind of dressing on them that we could close. Since it was now darker outside than in, each of the windows acted like a mirror, reflecting our cameras, lights, crew...everything.

Jackie had to explain to the Everains twice, why they didn't want the cameras picking up all that extra visual information.

At 11 o'clock that night, we left their house with no footage. At different points Jackie had attempted to shoot 'test footage' with the goal of using that for the promos, but the Everains wanted no one near the cameras and they stayed well away from any activity that looked like brewing beer.

Back at the hotel, I noticed that I had a voice mail on my cell phone. It was Tessa. "I met the record label owner for Roster X Records in the terminal flying to Denver. He loved our demo and he wants to hear us perform tomorrow before he flies to New York on Tuesday. Fly out to Charlemagne so we can perform a show for him at my friend's house tomorrow night at

9 PM and we might be able to make this happen."

All I had to do was fly back home to Los Angeles in the morning with my boss, somehow manage to become too sick to come to work that day, get home, pack for snow, pack my music gear and get myself to Denver where I could rent a car and drive myself through the snow to some mountain town I've never been to. After that, I'd only potentially be one showcase performance away from my dream of being a music artist signed to a major label.

No problem at all.

I hit reply and typed, "I'll be there."

Lindsey Falco
Sunday, 17 December 2006

Lindsey woke to the sound of eight-year old voices talking over one another and laughter. "It's too early in the morning for anyone to be that happy," she complained to herself after checking the bedside clock and realizing that it was only 7:30 in the morning.

Nevertheless, she climbed out of bed, showered and went downstairs.

Susan had made a large spread of pancakes, scrambled eggs, grits and toast laid out on the counter buffet style so Megan and her friends could fill their own plates with what they wanted before going back into the living room to eat.

"No bacon?" Lindsey complained.

"We don't do swine in this house. They're filthy animals," Susan answered.

"Don't feed me that mess, you hypocrite. You eat catfish and they're bottom dwellers," Lindsey mimed something trickling down, "feeding off of the organic matter that drifts down from upper layers of the water column. Now that's nasty."

"My friend called this morning," Susan said. "We're going to her place after breakfast so you two can talk. In the meantime, fix a plate and join me in the breakfast nook."

Lindsey waited her turn, stacked four pancakes on

a plate and sat with her sister in the nook. They could still hear the clamor of the eight year olds coming from the other room, but it was unlikely any of the kids would pick up what they were talking about.

"Any dreams?"

"No. No clue who the daddy is either."

"Do you think maybe it's Andros? You two seem to get along well now."

Lindsey had already considered that possibility since he was the only person she had dated who she was still in regular contact with, but while everyone knew that she and Andros had dated off and on for two and a half years and currently were close friends, few knew the circumstances of their final breakup.

"It's not him. Whoever my dream husband is, has a female cousin in Canada who was born and raised there. Andros' people are all in America," Lindsey told her, happy to move on to other candidates.

They emptied their plates in silence from then on and Susan drove them the 20-minute ride to her friend Imoleen Faire's house.

Upon meeting Imoleen, Lindsey found her appearance to be as exotic as her name. She had bone white blond hair that cascaded without a hint of curl halfway down her back, aquiline facial features and deep brown eyes that were all the more piercing from the contrast with her fair complexion. She seemed more to glide across the room, than to walk. Unlike most people, there was no rise and fall to her height as she stepped across the room.

After inviting Lindsey and Susan in, they settled down over coffee in Imoleen's living room. "Before we begin, let me give you a brief overview of my dealings in dreams and how I became a lucid dreamer." Imoleen sat down at her dinner table next to Lindsey and across from Susan.

"As a child, I used to have vicious nightmares bad enough to wake me up screaming and if I fell back to sleep straightaway after having one of those nightmares, I would return right back into it. I was so terrified that I'd often want to sleep with my parents until in fifth grade, I had come across a book that told me that I could cease nightmares by understanding the reason I was having them. From then on, whenever I woke from a nightmare, I'd try and process the reason why I had it and decipher any hidden meanings that might be represented. In time, I began to be able to 'tune in' to the nature of my dreams upon entering them and discovered that I could wake my self up before anything bad happened by sensing when I was in a nightmare rather than a dream."

"Was it nightmares that made your hair that color?"

A look of irritation flashed across Imoleen's face. "No. I was born this way."

"Sorry." Lindsey told Imoleen. Sensing a cold stare coming from her sister, she told Susan, "Sorry," with additional emphasis.

Imoleen continued. "Anyhow, I had no formal training from anyone, but my power in lucid dreaming was increasing and over time, I learned how to bring people into my dreams, create objects by will of thought, change people from women to men and back and shape entire landscapes into whatever I could conceive. Sometimes, the things I created defied physics as we know it, but those dreams were hard to retain because they were so far removed from reality as we know it. Somewhere along the line, I must have gained the attention of something. I had a dream where I didn't know I wasn't awake which in itself, never happened at that point and then, even though I was outside in my dream, everything went dark and I could feel the presence of something very evil there."

"How old were you?" Lindsey asked.

This time, Lindsey's question didn't seem to bother Imoleen. "I was 15 years old and I woke myself up immediately, but even this was different. This time, as I was leaving the dream, I could feel myself raise up out of it. Then the next night, I had a different dream, but with the same result. I wasn't aware that I was in a dream until everything went black, and I felt that same presence. Again, as I was leaving the dream, I felt my body elevate out of it."

"This happened continually for the next two weeks where almost nightly, I would have these dreams that ended with that presence stalking me. It all ended one night when, as I was forcing myself to wake, something shadowy grabbed me by the legs as I was rising up and began pulling me back down into the dream."

Lindsey let out an involuntary gasp at this potential

121

turn in one of her own dreams.

Imoleen paused for a moment, but when no questions came, continued. "I don't know how long I struggled against the thing, but when I finally broke its grip, I woke up gasping for air is if I hadn't been breathing during the exertion to wake up. I spent the next several nights trying to avoid going to sleep while preparing my mind for how I intended to fight this thing using light since it only seemed to appear in the dark, but I never had another dream like it since."

"Do you think that there is the possibility that the dreams are somehow connected to reality?" Lindsey asked.

"Define reality. I think that there might be a connection between your waking life and your dreams, sure. You may be aware of something subconsciously and the only way it knows how to communicate what it knows is through your dreams."

"Do you think I might die in real life if I die in my dreams?"

"I doubt it, but I haven't died in a dream. Even with the one with the shadow,

I don't know if I woke up gasping out of lack of breathing or from being out of breath because I was thrashing around in my sleep. I do think it would be a good idea for you to go into your next dream knowing as much as possible about what's going on. There may be clues if you look at the entire sequence of your dreams from different angles and peer into aspects of them that might be less obvious from a cursory glance."

"So, start from the beginning?"

"I'm afraid so."

Lindsey told Imoleen and Susan the sequence of events the dreams took on, beginning with her trip to Niagara Falls, which hotel they stayed at, what they did while they were there and ending with the abduction and then she gave background information she picked up from the dreams that she thought might help in some way, such as her daughter being seven years old and her marriage taking place roughly a year before they had a child.

"So you had absolutely no premonition that something might be up?" Imoleen asked.

"No. No stress. No tension. No sense that anyone was avoiding a topic. Nothing until my husband was supposed to pick us up at the airport. That's when my dream daughter, Melanie began acting strange and said that she didn't think her dad would make it and then she disappeared a few moments later. I was grabbed while trying to find her."

"No idea why they didn't grab you both at the same time?"

"Maybe there's only one kidnapper? I don't know."

Susan, who had been silent until now asked "If there was only one kidnapper, wouldn't it have made more sense to grab you first? Melanie would probably follow out of human nature."

"I have no idea what my dream husband does for a job though. Maybe he's some kind of spy or drug runner or something and that's why his family is being kidnapped," Lindsey finished.

Imoleen thought for a few moments. "Did you fall back on instincts once it became clear something was wrong that indicated some kind of training or instruction in what to do in case of this type of event? If you knew by reflex what to do and who to call in such an event, that would point towards your husband probably having the kind of job where kidnapping is a possibility and might give us an idea of where to begin looking for your answers in the waking world."

"Not really. In the dream I used some self-defense, but I took Mixed Martial Arts training in real life. I went up to a blue belt in that after a friend had been raped at knife-point in her condo. Other than that, I had no special skills or knowledge of what to do in that kind of situation. Basically, I was in a near panic and trying to cope."

"You mentioned that you were in Niagara Falls. Why?"

"His cousin lived near there. We were there to visit with her and she thought it would be more fun for Melanie if we stayed at a hotel right by the falls."

"Think hard Lindsey. Why would you and your daughter go visit his cousin and he not accompany you. The answers may come through in general conversations you had in the dream with his cousin."

Lindsey leaned back into the couch pillows and for the first time since arriving, noticed how tense she had been - sitting in a crouched position trying to get to the bottom of her dreams. She pushed into the between spots of her memories of her dreams. The quiet conversations that are usually so easily forgotten and answers were waiting. "We were all supposed to visit, but there was something with his job where, at the last minute, he couldn't go. That's why Melanie and I went without him."

"What did he tell you about his job."

"I don't remember that. I remember telling his cousin," Lindsey raised her head and looked into the corner of the room thinking for a second, "Tylene. That's her name. I remember telling Tylene about it. When we booked the trip, he had expected that he would have been out of his job by then, he was thinking of quitting, but his superior had no intention on letting him leave. She was exerting some kind of pressure on him and because of that, he decided that it would be best for all of us if he didn't outright quit just yet."

"What kind of man did you marry Lin?" Susan asked.

Lindsey shrugged. Between the dreams and her job, she was mentally tired from thinking so intently for the past two days. "What can I say, Susan? We were happy. I know that much."

Imoleen took a sip of her coffee, poured a little more into her cup from the pot to heat it up some and poured more sugar into it as she asked, "What side of Niagara were you on?"

"The Canadian side."

"Are you sure you weren't there to hide out from something or someone?"

"If so, it must have been planned way in advance.

I got the impression that the trip was planned a few months prior to us taking it and there was no conversation to hint at that theory."

"And you have no idea what his name might be? Did you notice your married name? Knowing his last name might help some."

"I'll have to think about that some more. Maybe I can remember signing something."

"What about phone calls? How did he sound on the phone?"

"Tired. Perhaps a little depressed that he couldn't be with us. When I asked how things were on his job, he never wanted to talk about it. Mostly, he wanted to know how we were doing and what we were up to. He said it cheered him up to hear it. I never got the sense of danger though for him or us. It came across like he had a normal job he didn't like, but wasn't able to get out of it just yet for some reason."

Imoleen felt that the situation, whatever it was, warranted Lindsey attempting to go into the dream armed. She spent the next few hours teaching Lindsey some mental prompts to use before going to bed to prime her subconscious and some techniques that Lindsey might be able to use to work around commonly known limitations in dreams and how to conjure up weaponry or other resources in the dreams if necessary.

"The only thing is," Imoleen finished, "is that I don't know how far outside of the bounds you can go if you are dreaming the future of your waking life. You're in territory I haven't charted if that's the case."

    Lindsey and Susan both thanked her and rode back to Susan's house in silence-deep in their individual thoughts and both wondering what Lindsey had gotten herself into.

Lucien Karr
Sunday, 17 December 2006

The knock on the door that changed the course of Lucien Karr's life came at 7:38 on a Saturday morning. Lucien was watching a cop show on TV that he had recorded and complained loudly of solicitors ruining the days of people who didn't want to buy whatever they were being sold, in hopes the person at the door would vacate before he answered.

As he turned the corner from the living room and made the last ten steps before taking the knob and turning it though, he could see the person still standing on the porch through the frosted glass that dominated the upper third of their front door. Lucien swung open the door with unnecessary force followed by an impatient, "What?"

The solicitor didn't seem disturbed by his reception and that aggravated Lucien all the more. Lucien frowned harder at the man.

"Is Conrad home?" The man asked.

The guy was about six inches shorter than Lucien, was way older and his air of calm emboldened Lucien. "It's seven-thirty in the morning. What's wrong with you?" Lucien asked.

Lucien couldn't place what changed exactly, but along with a slight change of expression on the man's face, something about the man suddenly scared him. "If your father is home, I'd like a word with him."

"My parents are away for the weekend."

The man looked past Lucien, into what little of the house was visible through the open door, then took in every window to see if there was an unnatural part in curtain or blind. When Lucien didn't react, the man reached into his back pocket and pulled out a card. "This is where I'm staying." He handed the card to Lucien. "Tell your dad that his brother James came by to tell him that our father is dead. The funeral is next Saturday."

Lucien was confused. He had grown up believing his dad was an only child. "I think you have the wrong house. My grandfather died when my dad was eight years old and my dad was an only child."

"He hasn't changed a bit, has he?" James shook his head. "You have two uncles and an aunt."

"If that's the case, why haven't we met before?" "You'll have to ask your dad why he broke contact with our whole family all those years ago."

Lucien didn't want to admit it, but the man bore a resemblance to his dad. He asked the man a few more questions about his dad and the man had plausible answers each time that were different from what he heard his dad tell, but similar. These two had some kind of past together.

"You know, you look a lot like your granddad. Only taller. You're what? A seven footer?"

"Yes."

"What's your name?" The man asked.

Lucien surprised himself by answering. He still

didn't want to trust the man.

"I'm your dad's oldest brother, James. Pleased to meet you." James extended a hand. Lucien hesitated a moment, but shook it. "There's another brother before your dad, named Logan and a younger sister named Veronica."

"Look," James continued, "if you want, you can swing by the house I'm staying at or call me. Either way, we'd like to get to know you better, but I have to go. There are some others I need to notify in person about our father."

Lucien said, "Okay, I will." He put the card with James' address and phone number on it, in his wallet, then shut the door on the departing figure of his new-found uncle. He sat back down to watch his cop show with dozens of questions circulating in his head.

When the show was over, he went into his parent's bedroom and stood in the doorway. The bed was made and decorated with five extra pillows of assorted size and shape with patterns that complimented the comforter and matching shams.

On their dresser, was a picture from a family cruise they had taken the year before to the Bahamas. Lucien entered their room and picked it up. They were seated in a cafe with a linoleum floor at a table with a single fish on each of their plates.

They had made a pact with each other that day to try something new and agreed eating a fish that was served with its dead eyes still in its head qualified.

They had laughed and cringed and enjoyed the meal even though they weren't too eager to repeat it. Returning to the ship, they came across the same children on the dock that they had as they came off of it offering to sing a song for a dollar. Lucien's mom convinced his dad to give one of the children two dollars to sing two songs. The child sang what sounded like two verses before insisting he had sang two songs. Lucien's dad was afraid the boy had some form of protection nearby to enforce for the children, so he let it go until they were back on the ship where he could safely complain how he was ripped off.

Lucien had just turned 18 years old, so while the ship was in international waters, he and his dad would stop by some of the cruise ship bars and have drinks together. They talked about women, sports and the finer points of accounting since his dad knew much more about numbers than he did the other two subjects. It was the most grown up that Lucien had ever felt up to that point.

He set the picture back down on the dresser, careful to place it in the position he found it. He walked to the closet and slid open the door. He pulled down a shoebox off of the top shelf. The weight of it surprised him, and whatever the thing was in the box, slide along the bottom, bumping to a stop along an inside corner. Lucien cradled the box in one arm and opened it. There was a revolver inside along with a box of bullets. Fearful of the weapon, Lucien replaced the box top and gently set it back on the closet shelf.

He pulled down every other box in the closet, one at a time, and had rummaged through every drawer in the room without a trace of what he was looking for. Since he had the whole weekend before his parent's return, he searched the entire house and found no photos of his dad's childhood. The photos he did find were all taken after his parents had married, but didn't include any of the actual ceremony which he was told took place at a city hall in Maryland.

When his parents returned home, he tried to subtly question them both about their history before marriage, but the same stories kept getting recycled as if they were talking points from a politician. He considered calling or going by to visit James to get more answers, but he was shy about finding more about his mystery relatives until he got more perspective from his dad.

Something had happened between them, and considering that his mom and dad had been loving and supportive of Lucien his entire life, he was still inclined to trust his dad's reasoning for breaking ties with his family even if he didn't know what the reasoning was.

By the day of the funeral, Lucien still wasn't ready to confront his dad or consult with his uncle, so he took in a movie with a friend and pretended everything was normal.

This pretense of normality continued for four more months before Lucien stood on the doorstep of the house bearing the address he had kept on a card in his wallet all that time. He rapped knuckle on door and waited.

Seconds later an old man was staring at him through the cracked open door, wide eyed. "You're the boy James spoke of. Gerald's grandson."

Lucien nodded his head, unsure of how to proceed. The man put his hand out for a shake. "I'm Milford. Friend of your grandfather.

During the war, I kept his P-38 Lightning airborne in the Pacific Theater." Milford shuffled backwards and opened the door further. "Come in, son. Come in."

Lucien came through the door and knew from the smell that James didn't live there. The house bore the stuffy scent of old wood and paper tinged with liniment that seemed to linger in every old person's dwelling he had ever been in.

"Is James here?" Lucien asked even though he expected a negative.

"No, son. His emergency leave was up long ago."

"Emergency leave?"

"He's Navy. Ex-SEAL. At his age, he's more administrative now. Body can't take the same bumps and shocks after putting SEAL miles on it all those years." Milford led Lucien into a small kitchen with a circular table pushed into a corner of it. There were two chairs with vinyl floral patterned cushions on them, placed sideways to the table, backs each touching one of the two walls the table was bumped up against. He motioned for Lucien to take one. "Have a seat son. Coffee?"

"Uh, sure."

Milford pulled a coffee mug down from a cupboard and turned to a stovetop coffee percolator making a glurping sound over a low fire from the stove burner. He poured a cup of coffee for Lucien, put a little more coffee in his own mug, then topped off his drink with a splash of bourbon. He stirred it with a wrinkled finger. He noticed Lucien watching him. "Keeps heat in my bones, you see." he said.

"I'm not sure why I'm here."

Milford set creamer and sugar on the table for Lucien, then sat on the other chair at the table. "Because you're curious where you came from. It's natural you want to know your kin. You have two cousins living local. Most everyone else of an age is serving."

"Serving?"

"Military. Goes way back in your blood. Your father is the first male Karr not to serve since Rutherford B. Hayes was President. Even your women took to enlisting, but your daddy was made from different stuff. He tried, mind you, but washed out of Basic."

"You know my dad?"

"I know all your people. Gerald was like my brother. His kids, like my own, of a sort." Milford brought his mug up to his mouth and slurped. "Your daddy wasn't much for things requiring physical coordination, but he was a regular abacus. Could run numbers in his head like nobody else I ever knew. Gerald was proud of him, but never knew how to make Conrad believe it though. A man like your grandaddy kept the feeling part mostly on the inside and after all the kids but your daddy was in uniform, he took more to them with conversation. He just understood them better.

Conrad went radio silent not long after."

"Where was my grandmother?"

Milford raised his head in dreamy eyed remembrance. "Ethel Mae Karr passed when your daddy was eight. Robbery went bad and she got the worst of it. Well, her and two others outside my acquaintance. It was just your grandaddy wearing the pants and the apron strings after. He was a vet by that time, working electrical for the city of L.A."

Milford anchored a hand on the table, another on his chair and pushed himself to standing. Grabbed his mug with one hand and turned the low flame burning on the stove off. "Follow me." The swish of his slippers sounded on the tile floor as he made for the door and Lucien followed, the smell of the place not as strong as it was.

Milford's pace was slow, allowing Lucien to take in the old pictures, water color paintings and plaques with inspirational quotes hanging on the walls. "Is this your wife?" Lucien asked, stopping next to a black and white photograph of a 20-something year old brunette woman wearing a dark dress and staring at something to the left of the photographer.

"That's my Mildred. We were together 46 years before God wanted her with him more than with me. Used pneumonia to take her." Milford turned abruptly away and continued down the dark hallway into his bedroom.

"Nice bedroom set," Lucien said.

Milford beamed a bit. "Solid Oak. The lot of it. Made to last, like me. Now come over here and quit changing the subject. I want to show you this." Milford picked up a framed photo with a younger version of him in it.

He was wearing a cap with ear flaps standing next to a plane with two fuselages, his smile as wide as the horizon. Standing next to him, was a man bearing Lucien's hawk nose and deep set eyes.

"This was taken shortly after Frank Edwards took over your grandaddy's squadron. Frank was studying theology with plans for the ministry when Hitler and Japan got too big for their britches and he traded school books for a yoke. He got on a lot about how the pilots needed to hunt the Oscars, Zeros and Vals like a pack of wolves. You see, Frank wanted team effort in taking out the enemy and your granddaddy took that notion of team to heart with a fierceness even after discharge. Family and friends formed the pack and you held together, but your daddy didn't feel like a fit, so he left. I hope you see what I'm getting at."

"I think I do."

"Good. Because you've got to be part of something larger. Family. Friends. Something. You can't make it in this world alone. I know some try and think they have it figured. Until a real pack crosses their path and they realize they're outnumbered and surrounded by an enemy."

*****

That's exactly what Lucien felt - surrounded by enemies.

For the first time since the party, he was able to work his way out of the bed and the dried up filth he was laying in. He still felt overly fatigued and even though he doubted he would ever be able to prove it, he was sure he had been drugged in some way. Hangovers didn't feel like this no matter how much Peter claimed he had drank that night.

After getting himself washed and free of the pine tar and feathers, Lucien checked the bedroom door and found it locked. Next, he tried both windows in the room, but both only opened to a seven-story drop to the cement below. There was no ledge he could hope to use as an escape route.

He returned to the bathroom and sat down on the toilet seat cover thoroughly winded. Once he had regained a little strength, he got up and checked the medicine cabinet looking for a pair of scissors, a razor or some other makeshift weapon he could procure and hide on his person in case it became needed or an escape presented itself, but it was empty.

He sat on the toilet and looked at the feathers on the floor and lingering around the bathroom. He hated the sight of them and considered cleaning them up just to remove them from sight, but then he remembered that he was a prisoner and he didn't want to do anything to aid his jailor.

He went back into the bedroom and took the seat Gaelle had occupied when he first woke up. Normally, he tried not to think of how his life might have been different if his parents hadn't separated him from the rest of his family and more importantly, hadn't ingrained a sense of awkwardness into him. From his earliest memory on, his parents had always preached that his clumsiness had been inherited and that it would forever make him a social outcast, but that it wasn't his fault. It was Milford that challenged those ideas after tales of Lucien's childhood had grown a sense of disgust in Milford so strong, that Milford decided to put Lucien's alleged ineptitude to the test.

That was when Lucien first picked up a brush and began painting in water color. Milford had learned it at the local senior center and taught Lucien how to paint to prove Lucien's parents wrong.

"If you can't control your limbs, you can't paint," Milford told Lucien three weeks in to their daily lessons. They were standing in front of the first of Lucien's canvases that mirrored the image he first envisioned in his mind.

From there, Milford added pencil and charcoal illustration to Lucien's curriculum. The whole while, Lucien kept his new skill a secret from his parents, telling them that he was being mentored by a retired engineer from an aerospace company.

He had learned so much from Milford, but with all of his help and good intentions, Milford couldn't completely undo all the damage that Lucien's parents had done. Now, Lucien was a prisoner because the huge strides he made in creating art didn't translate to his ability to socialize with the ease he had hoped to one day gain.

***

Lucien sat there for an hour chastising his poor choice of crashing a party in an attempt to win over a girl that wasn't even there as far as he remembered.

He was so busy berating his stupidity, that he didn't notice the sound of a key being inserted into the locked door. He looked up as the door swung open and Peter entered the room. "Good. You're dressed. Come on out. I can't talk in here with the smell."

Lucien rose and slowly followed Peter out into a hallway that was wide enough for three grown men to walk down it abreast without worry of brushing up against a wall. One of Peter's friends was just outside the door and with Peter leading the way, his friend followed behind Lucien. A few seconds later, the name Seth came to him. He had met Seth at the party before his memory of the evening's events went dark.

As they walked, Lucien began having snippets of conversation glance through his mind from the party. Still these were all from the first hour of his visit. His attempts to recall a pool game or anything regarding the feathers, failed. His initial reaction to the vast array of stuffed animals in the apartment was returning with unease. There were at least a dozen more dead trophies situated on shelves built into the hall walls, but these were smaller creatures. An owl. A coiled rattlesnake. An armadillo.

Amidst the taxidermy, were weaponry. An ancient axe with the stone blade tied to a wooden post with a sinewy material. A small variety of blowguns. A few war hammers. He considered the likelihood of using any of the objects in the hall to overtake Peter and Seth, but given his sapped strength, he wasn't sure he could raise anything capable of delivering real damage up over his head to bring it down with any force.

He took a closer look at Peter who was a foot shorter, but was lean with muscle and his stride bore a certain belligerence as if he tended towards anger. Lucien didn't think he could take Peter on in a fight even if he weren't outnumbered and impaired.

Peter led them into his living room. There were deer antlers everywhere. The wall sconces were made from them, the chandelier hanging over the coffee table was made out of them, and there were spare sets as kill trophies adorning all of the walls. "Sit down." Peter said pointing at the leather couch on the other side of the cof-fee table from the leather couch he sat down on. Seth remained standing and circled behind the couch Lucien sat down on.

Lucien gestured at the vast array of dead animal remains being used as decoration. "Did you kill all of these yourself?"

Peter clasped his hands together. "Look. Before you can go on your merry way, I need some answers."

"Will I get my phone and wallet back, then?"

"If I'm happy. If I'm not happy, you won't be either."

Lucien watched him closely as he spoke, looking for any kind of tell that might indicate what Peter might have planned for him, but saw nothing. "Okay. What do you want to know?"

"Why did you break into my place?"

The truth was there for Lucien, but shame was larger and meaner, so the truth cowered down into a corner. He started to turn to see what Seth was doing behind him, but Peter cautioned against that, so Lucien turned back forward.

"If you weren't here to cause harm, you have nothing to worry about."

"I was locked in a room the past two days."

"As opposed to me tying weights on your body and dropping you over the side of my yacht twenty miles off the coast of California. Not a bad second choice, I'd say. What do you think, Seth?"

"He got the choice I'd pick."

Peter raised his hands in a gesture that the obvious was just announced. "See? Besides, do you give uninvited guests the run of your home?"

"No."

"Exactly. So, an answer, while I'm still being understanding."

"I was passing by and heard the music. It seemed like the thing to do at the time. You've never crashed a party before?"

"Never had to." Peter said, impatience flashing across his face. "I'll ask again. Why my place? And, don't lie. I'll knock out all your teeth and mount them on my wall."

Between his looks and his money, Lucien didn't figure Peter had any trouble attracting women, so he felt a warm rush of humiliation creep up his features as he admitted, "There was an American Indian girl who I thought came in this building and was attending your party. She had shown interest in me until I had embarrassed myself in front of her earlier in the evening. I was hoping to win her back over."

From there, it was an interrogation that lasted an hour as Lucien and Seth returned to the same questions over and over again, but from different angles trying to confuse Lucien. In some cases, Lucien floundered and was lost in the cadence of their rapid fire questioning bouncing off of his answers, but he didn't lie and both Peter and Seth eventually seemed satisfied that he wasn't there to do any harm, whatever they meant by that.

"Okay. I think this might work to both our advantage." Peter said, tapping a finger on his thigh, still formulating a plan.

"What might work?" Lucien asked.

"I have a situation you can help me with while benefitting yourself."

Lucien wanted to tell him, "No," because he had no doubt that Peter was going to come out far ahead of him in whatever transaction Peter was cooking up. "What do I need to do?" He asked instead.

"Hold on." Peter reached into his pocket and pulled out his cell phone and quick-dialed someone.

"Answer me this. Is she pregnant? Because you can't be so stupid as to think this is why I gave you the use of my private plane for your birthday," was the greeting Peter received.

"No one is pregnant."

"Good. So why did you put some woman on my plane and send her to Turkey using my plane?"

"I think we've established whose plane it is, dad."

"Have we? Because you aren't acting like it's not your plane?"

"It was a trade."

"A trade!? With whom? Why?"

"It's better you don't know yet."

"What does that mean?"

"It will become apparent soon. Until then, you don't want to know."

"You really do want Behrendt Airways to go to your sister, don't you?"

"Dad! Listen for a minute. The person who used your plane put me in touch with an artist who can paint the murals you wanted in your business class lounges."

"You traded an international flight on my plane for a phone number for someone who probably waits tables when he isn't finger painting? You can't possibly be my son. Even if my sperm had suffered some form of trauma from your mother's hostile eggs, it couldn't account for you."

Peter let out an exasperated sigh. "Can you meet with the artist and I on Monday, dad? Yes or no."

Peter waited while his dad checked his schedule. "Noon then. At Spoilers."

Peter said, "Okay, we'll see you there," to a dead line. While putting the phone back in his pocket, he told Lucien, "You're staying here one more night. Non-negotiable. After the meeting with my dad," he raised and pointed a finger at Lucien, "where you'll agree to paint murals for Berendt Airways business class lounges for a reasonable fee, you'll be free to go."

"It didn't seem like your dad is interested. What if he says no?"

Seth had come around the couch and sat next to Lucien. "He won't. We saw your work at the gallery while you were out of commission."

Lucien blushed slightly over the compliment. "I still don't understand how this softens up you using his plane. What were you planning on doing before I came through the window?"

"Something less distracting and you don't have to understand what's going on. Just play your part," Peter said.

"Is this about Gaelle? Is she the woman he's talking about?" Lucien asked.

Peter shook his head as if he was ready to be finished with the conversation and was losing patience that it wasn't over yet. He gave a look to Seth and Lucien caught the slight nod of Seth's head as a reply before Peter answered, "She said she thinks you're nice and that she liked you. If you feel the same about her, you'll pretend you know nothing about her being on that plane."

"Doesn't she have to go through customs? There's still a trail."

Peter leaned forward conspiratorially, "Not with the passport she's using."

Lucien felt Seth reach around his back and clutch his far shoulder. Seth drew him in close. Lucien did his best not to frown at the stink from the mix of diet soda and Brussels sprouts on Seth's breath as Seth told him, "Let's just say, out of the few people who knows where Gaelle disappeared to, you're the only link that could be considered weak."

Aristotle Troublefield
Sunday, 17 December 2006

Aristotle forcefully stabbed the last bite of toaster-heated waffle with his fork and shoved it into his mouth. He chewed it with aggression while casting a mean stare at the inanimate objects in Epistrophy's kitchen.

He was still outraged over what happened at Peter's party, but was thinking that he should probably make up with Sandy in case Gloon started screwing him over. It was just good business to have a personal tie to the founder of the company that parented his record label. All he had to do was figure out how not to care about her feelings.

He stood up, grabbed his dish and tossed it into the sink where it could lay with the sink full of dishes Epistrophy had dirtied, but wouldn't clean until there were no dishes left in drawer or cupboard to use. Sandy had complained about the clutter in the house one too many times during the two months they had been dating, so he stopped having her over. While it was true that he wasn't as bad as Epistrophy, the situation still translated into him spending more time at her place and her complaining about the clutter he left there.

Aristotle picked up his notebook full of poems and tried to write, but nothing came to him except an annoying urge to clean up his bedroom.

Her influence was all over his life and he resented

that. He turned on the television and let the channel rest on a college football game. Thankfully, neither of the teams on the field represented the university she attended, so he half watched the game and half considered anything he could to crowd thoughts of Sandy out of his mind.

He wondered if he should have let her take him home the other night and explain her side of the story. He was doing a show here and there for the label and bringing in a little money, but was still a ways away from creating an album with enough potential hits that Dawn Mega was going to be willing to release it. Until that happened and he started touring behind it, he couldn't afford to replace the clothes and other things he had left at her place.

He berated himself as an idiot for lowering his guard long enough to put himself in this position. The only suit he owned was at her place along with most of his other nice clothes. Even some of his stage clothes were there since he usually finished gig nights at her spot.

"Wassup?" Epistrophy asked as he came in the house.

"Same plantation, different whip," Aristotle answered back. He made sure he was facing Epistrophy so that Epistrophy could read his lips.

One of the first things Aristotle learned about Epistrophy was that the headphones he kept wrapped around his ears all of the time was to drown out the tinitus he began to suffer from, beginning at the age of 18, because of an abnormal bone growth near both of his middle ears called otosclerosis. He had inherited the disease from his mother who kept earbuds in her ears to drown out her own tinitus.

He took the name Epistrophy because that was his mom's favorite song from her favorite artist, Thelonious Monk. She liked to claim that while she was pregnant with Epistrophy, she wore the vinyl grooves down so bad, where the song appeared on Thelonious Monk's Septet, she had to buy another copy.

His entire immediate family knew sign language and read lips so that they communicate with others without having to remove their headphones or yell at each other. Aristotle was originally jealous of how loving and supportive Epistrophy's family was to each other, but quickly got over it when they extended that sense of belonging over to him when they didn't have to.

Now, I either betray the closest thing I have to family or get dropped from my record label and become unemployed again, Aristotle thought to himself. He kept the disgust he felt over his situation off of his face and asked Epistrophy, "Wassup with you?"

"Chilling. Didn't expect to see you here on a weekend. You and your girl fighting?"

"Why is that the first place you go?"

"If I'm wrong, just say no. Any word about what's up with your next CD? I've written over twenty beats for it, it's time to get in the studio."

Aristotle made a face and turned back to the TV.

Epistrophy shrugged and left the room.

The game was almost over when Aristotle's phone rang and he was as aggravated at the part of himself that hoped it was Sandy as he was at the part of him that was relieved that it wasn't her.

"We're at your curb. Come outside dressed for a ride."

"Who is this?" Aristotle asked.

"Gloon, Maaaaannn. Tomorrow, we start in the studio, but today, we start on your record. You got five minutes before my man Hughy here kicks in your door and carries you out."

Aristotle parted the living room curtains and saw two black Chevy Tahoes parked outside of the house with a couple bodybuilder types, what looked like four kids in their late teens and Gloon all standing around the SUVs.

Aristotle realized that if Epistrophy saw Gloon and his entourage outside his house, there would be no way to delay telling him about being replaced as producer and demoted to a beat maker having to go through a gatekeeper to get his music approved for inclusion on Aristotle's album. He ran into his bedroom, grabbed a pair of shoes and happily managed to avoid Epistrophy as he ran outside in his socks, thinking maybe Gloon's intrusion wouldn't be disastrous.

"Okay, let's go." He told Gloon and his associates as he ran across the front lawn carrying his shoes.

He saw the smirks passing between Gloon and the others, but Gloon ordered everyone into the SUVs ending any discussion on the matter. "You ride up front with me."

Gloon told Aristotle and motioned at the passenger seat in the first of the two Tahoes.

Two of the teenagers got in the backseat.

"Are they your kids?" Aristotle asked, gesturing his head towards the back seat as he put his shoes on.

"You really don't do your homework do you?" Gloon stopped what he was doing to ask. "These are my lead interns. Every year, my foundation runs a contest and chooses eight kids from inner cities to shadow me for 11 months of work. After that time, my staff places them to produce or engineer indie music projects my foundation selects from inner city recording artists, allowing them to record in a low key, decently equipped studio at my home base in Atlanta."

"The bodybuilders?"

"Bodyguards."

"Should I have also figured out where we're going?"

"Were your parents church goers?"

"We're going to church?"

"Answer my question, I'll answer yours."

"No. Pops would go to the bar and watch sports with his friends all day. Moms would be about the house."

"No. We're not going to church."

Gloon honked once, the SUV behind them honked once back, then he pulled out from the curb.

"You never said where we're going?" Aristotle reminded him.

"We're going to let me ask the questions for the rest of today."

Aristotle resisted the urge to fold his arms across his chest and watched the sights pass by as he tried to piece together where Gloon was taking him.

After fifteen minutes into their journey, his thoughts segued back to Sandy and how close he came to being drugged, tarred and feathered. There was a pressure point that the whole thing struck that he didn't think he could communicate to her and the more he thought about it, the more he wondered if he wanted to.

Forty minutes later, they pulled up to a house Aristotle didn't recognize. It was a single story house that looked like most of the other single story homes on the block. There was a large fence that ran in front of the homes dividing the homes from the bridal trail that took the space a sidewalk normally would have. Further up the block someone was on a horse using the trail.

As they walked up the driveway past a late model silver Corvette, Aristotle took in the crisp, manicured green lawn, the two boulders placed as if by design in the front yard to accentuate the purple, yellow and white flowers growing around the base of a birch tree.

The house had two large garden windows on either side of a huge porch peeking out from its frame with more flowers growing just inside. Aristotle wondered if this was Gloon's home until one of the bodyguards knocked on the door.

Aristotle was toward the rear of the group and

couldn't see much beyond the upper portion of the door as it opened wide and everyone started filing in.

The person who opened the door must have been leading the group into wherever they were going in the house, but Gloon and one of his bodyguards was right by Aristotle's side as he crossed the threshold. Gloon closed the door behind him.

The house smelled of Christmas tree pine and Aristotle looked for pictures to place the homeowner as they filed deeper into the house, but only found artwork on the walls. The procession was eerily devoid of conversation, creating an uncomfortable juxtaposition to the bright, welcoming home they were in and when they reached the living room where Gloon's people were already taking seats, he saw sitting next to each other on a sectional couch holding hands, his parents.

He almost didn't recognize them. They both looked happier and healthier than he had ever seen them and the shock of realizing that the turnaround was most likely his absence filled him with a self loathing that paralyzed him where he stood. He wanted to ask Gloon why he was doing this. He wanted to know why this couldn't have been the type of environment his parents raised him in rather than Primrose, a suburb of Los Angeles nicknamed "Grimrose" by the residents due to the crime and drugs running rampant through the streets. He wanted to know what was so wrong with him that they couldn't even conceive of having nice things until he was absent. All these thoughts coupled with the questions he couldn't put to words and crushed him in a way that made him wish he had the will to once again move his body, so he could kill himself.

Aristotle only vaguely felt powerful hands take a grip of his shoulders and guide him to a seat.

Gloon was in front of him then, snapping fingers as if that would remove the spell of his shock. The words, "Why would I be?" came out of Aristotle without conscious effort when Gloon asked if he was alright.

They stayed at that place for an amount of time Aristotle couldn't keep track of, with Gloon seemingly interviewing his parents. Parts of their discussion seeped into Aristotle's awareness, such as how his dad Cyrus Troublefield, never wanted a child and took to heavy drinking and general belligerence until Aristotle's mother kicked Aristotle out of the house at gunpoint while Aristotle was a 16-year old junior in high school. After Aristotle was gone, Cyrus began going to AA meetings and the couple started down a road of healing. In time, the romance returned to their marriage with discoveries of new interests like riding horses and between his con-struction work and her new found career as an adminis-trative assistant, they were able to put themselves in a position financially to move out of the poor neighbor-hood Aristotle kept them in and buy a horse property to stable the 'his' and 'hers' horses they bought each other one Valentine's Day.

Aristotle's fog never fully lifted and more was said about his parent's remarkable recovery of a life well lived without the burden of him being part of it, but at some point, Aristotle's mind clicked off as a mercy. He didn't even have the strength to cry, in spite of a deep seated need to.

When Gloon had pulled all the information he wanted from his parents, Aristotle felt his body lifted up and over the shoulder of one of the bodyguards before being gently placed in the front seat of one of the Tahoes. He only barely registered that it was now nighttime.

When they arrived back at Epistrophy's house, he was once again lifted up and out by a bodyguard. He vaguely remembered being swung over a muscular shoulder while someone knocked at the door. At some point, he was set down on the couch. There was a reminder that he needed to be at the studio at a quarter to eight in the morning. Something was said about fifty pushups that sounded like a threat.

The emotional tornado cutting a swath through his psyche was so noisy that he was only partially able to register the anger and betrayal present in Epistrophy's voice when his best friend, current landlord, and now, ex-producer stood over his prone figure and asked him if there was something he needed to know about the recording of Aristotle's next CD.

Andros Koresh
Monday, 18 December 2006

No one was happy, least of all, me. We had spent a tension filled, two hours past our take off time waiting at our gate in Portland for the airline to fix a seat that was broken on our aircraft. As soon as the people with children and disabilities were allowed to board, Jackie announced, "I spoke to Rodrick and due to the delay, he wants us to come in to work directly from the airport. You'll all be dropped off at your residences after work today instead of before. Sorry." Then she hid her face back behind her magazine.

Chaz grumbled something about an all-around amateur hour, Araceli continued using a nanny cam she had placed in her backpack to record irritated passengers while we waited and Jeremy turned his iPod back up. The wrinkles in his young frown deepened. I pulled my cell phone back out and dialed my friend Truck.

He greeted me with, "The answer is no."

"You haven't heard my question yet."

"I already went by your apartment this morning before work, at a moment's notice I might add, to grab your snow clothes and throw them in a bag. The bag's in my car and you're welcome to come get it. The answer would change to yes if you're about to ask if your place looks trashed and your acoustic guitar is broken beyond repair. That diva of yours has a temper. If your question falls outside the parameters of the topics I just covered, then ask, otherwise you have your answer."

"I won't have my car before I have to leave for the airport today. We're going directly from LAX to Razor[Gun]. Is there really no way you can get my stuff to me there. Time is tight and I don't want to screw myself out of this opportunity."

There was a long pause, so I asked, "How often do I ask for favors like this?"

The pause continued, but there was nothing more for me to say.

"I'll get them to your building. By what time?"

"Anytime before 1 PM if you can also drive me to the airport."

"How about a foot massage while we're at it?" Truck said this loud enough for everyone within a three seat radius of me to hear.

The gate attendants called our zone to board, so I slung my computer bag across my shoulder. "No foot massage. I'd just feel dirty, but is that a yes for the ride?"

"You will owe me. And I mean big."

"It's a long lunch for you. You're in charge. It's your outfit. Who's to complain?"

"I'll be at Razor[Gun] at 12:30."

"You're the best friend ever."

He called me a name that children would get swatted for saying and hung up. I boarded and after finding my seat, I texted Tessa that I would need to borrow a guitar, then realized as I turned my phone off that she should already know that since our set was supposed to be unplugged and she broke my acoustic guitar. A groundswell of anger crept back into my vision of the future and I immediately started stamping out the fire growing in my gut before it grew too large to put out.

I didn't want petty issues to stand between me and the opportunity to be signed to a label like Roster X. For three years straight, their short list of artists had all charted because of the keen ear and work ethic of Trea Shar the Terrasonic, their primary in-house producer. If Tessa and I were able to work with him, that would be an amazing next chapter in our recording careers.

As I contemplated this, Chaz complained loud enough for everyone in the cabin to hear him say, "The plane is only half full. Why didn't they just fix the broken seat once we were in Los Angeles?"

A flight attendant was by his seat in seconds, counseling him to settle down.

Chaz told him, "While you're here, how about a Jim Beam. Neat. That always settles me down. Thanks."

The flight attendant appeared paralyzed for a few seconds, probably wondering like I was, if the outburst was for the sole intention of garnering a drink before the rest of the cabin was being served. When the flight attendant began moving again, he went to go get Chaz his drink.

I changed seats to sit next to Chaz. In spite of my efforts to get myself to Charlemagne to do the showcase with Tessa, I was still conflicted about going and I wanted advice from someone who had been successful in the entertainment field.

I told Chaz what was going on, let him know that I was trying to avoid being a complete idiot and showed him the text. He gave my thigh a good smack, accompanied by, "Break a leg."

He mimed wrapping duct tape around his head to gag his mouth when I warned him not to tell Jackie or anyone else that I was going to finish my day in Colorado instead of California. I wasn't sure what excuse I was going to use yet, but it was definitely going to involve a lie of some kind.

Chaz' drink had arrived while I was telling my story, but he didn't touch it until I was done. When he did pick it up, he drank it straight out of the mini bar bottle, bypassing the plastic cup he was given and then swished it around in his mouth.

"What are you doing? It isn't mouthwash," I said.

He continued with the swishing as if I hadn't said anything, then after swallowing, said, "It's called the Kentucky Chew. Different parts of your mouth pick up different flavors of the bourbon. The Kentucky Chew helps you taste them." He smiled. "It also brings out some of the bite in the flavors."

"What's with you and alcohol anyways? Every time I turn around you have a drink in your hand."

"Did you ever see my movie *Renquist?*"

I shook my head.

"You should rent it. Anyways, a lot of the relationships

that came into play during the making of that film were
formed at parties. Some public. Some private. That, of
course, translated into steady and ready access to copious
amounts of drugs and alcohol, which I was cool with, but my
wife...wellllll, she didn't so much like the stuff as need it."

Chaz began to fumble with the bottle. "It wasn't a
big deal at first, but as time wore on, she got worse and
worse. I wasn't seeing this though, I was on location.
Here and there, I'd get a phone call from a friend or
neighbor that she didn't pick the kids up from school or
she crashed the car into something, but it was my first
time directing a $100 million film, and all my energy was
focused on making it a success."

Chaz looked straight ahead. I waited. "I took care
of myself and my career for another film, which came to
two more years before she got sloppy enough with her
habit, that our youngest daughter found some of my
wife's cocaine, and thinking it was sugar, put it on her
breakfast cereal." Chaz paused. His eyes were glassy now.

"Thankfully, our oldest son had taken to parenting
his younger brother and sister in my wife's and my
absence, recognized the innocent looking container my
wife kept her blow in and stopped his sister from eating
it." Chaz raised his eyebrows in wonder. "It was him, our
oldest, that coordinated the intervention for my wife. I
flew home for it. She chose to get clean and I put her in a
rehab facility."

"On my flight back to where we were filming, it
occurred to me that rehab would only help her get

sober. For her to stay sober, we'd have to change our friends, our lifestyle and my job. That's why I retired from film directing after Love Me Not, we moved to a new neighborhood and I took this job. I know. I know. You asked about my drinking. Not all this other stuff, but without context, no tale of sacrifice is understood. So. About my drinking. I enjoy the taste of certain alcohols, so I allow myself a single alcoholic drink a day when I'm away from my wife and I relish it. If there wasn't such a stigma over drinking, you would have noticed that I enjoy my food equally." He patted his slightly bulging belly. He turned his body to face me. "Obviously, I'd appreciate if this remained between us."

"Yeah. Sure." I said, then I had to ask, "There was no way you could have stayed directing and just kept her away from the drugs?"

"Not safely." He leaned his seat back and closed his eyes. "If you'll pardon me, I'll be taking a nap now."

I leaned my own seat back thinking about what Chaz had just told me and the next thing I knew, we had landed and people were already pulling their belongings out of the overhead bins.

I grabbed my things and joined the broken line of people making their way to the checked baggage carousel.

I was barely able to keep my eyes open after my nap, and part of me wondered how well I would fare once I landed in Denver and then had to drive through the snow covered Rocky Mountains to reach

Charlemagne. I gave my head a vigorous shake, but the mental sluggishness persisted.

With a minimum of conversation, we collected our things and Jackie drove us all back to Razor[Gun]. As we all climbed out of the mini-van, Chaz asked the questions, "We don't have to lug all of our personal stuff through security, do we? Can't we leave it in the van?"

"Leave it if you like!" Jackie snapped at him.

They left every bag not carrying Razor[Gun] equipment in the van. I took my luggage and gear bag both, claiming that I was afraid the van would be broken into and as I watched a building security guard go through them both checking for weapons or indications of explosives, I cursed Russell Ferguson. He was the tenant who inspired enough hatred that his life was in perpetual danger. After personally putting up the money to cover the cost of the additional security personnel manning the entrance lobby, he was allowed to lease space in the building, much to all of the other tenant's inconvenience.

Because of the additional search my personal luggage required, I was the last one to make it up to our offices. Jackie had already been summoned into a closed door meeting with Rodrick. I cursed her too. I needed to meet with Rodrick myself to coordinate the terms of my escape.

I checked the gear back into Supply that I needed for Portland before finding my seat.

Eva appeared in front of my desk as I negotiated where to put my personal luggage so it wouldn't be in my way. "Is the witch dead, or do you think her flying monkeys will somehow save her?" She asked looking in the direction of Rodrick's office.

I woke up my computer and called up a video graphic file for a station ID that I needed to have done before leaving for Charlemagne. "I don't know. She's been quiet since everything fell apart yesterday. Maybe Lindsey is off the hook. By the way, where is she?"

"She went out for lunch. Did she tell you about the guy that she's wedding bells into--."

"Since when was Lindsey into marriage?" I tried to keep my voice even and natural, but there was a pang inside me at the thought that Lindsey was having thoughts of marriage.

"I don't know." After my unexpected reaction, Eva wore a frown of worry that she may have said too much. "I better get back to the editing bay." She was gone before I could protest.

I pulled open a couple of my desk drawers searching, before I found a piece of card stock paper I could write on. I wrote a quick note on it, folded it in half so it would tent, and left it standing on the computer keyboard in Lindsey's office.

I was more hurt than I knew I had a right to be. When she and I ended as a couple all those years ago, she was dead set against marriage. Something had changed in her and I missed it entirely. Some friend, I thought.

I put some finishing touches on my motion graphic

file and started the rendering process that would take the forty-eight sound and graphic files I used to create the station ID and turn it into a single video file ready for broadcast. The software estimated that it would take an hour to complete.

Rendering used most of my computer's resources, so while it was tied up with rendering, I picked up one of my sketchbooks and continued my concept work for a hotel branding package I was part of the team on.

I was still doing my mind map of keyword associations for the project when Lindsey appeared. She had a slight bump over one eye, with puffy eyes from a very recent cry. She looked raw and since we were in the office, I didn't want to accidentally encourage a new burst of tears. I decided to let her choose the topic.

"So that's the new campaign, huh?" She asked in greeting. She pointed at some of the Everain posters I had laying on my desk. I was done with them, but kept them visible. It was part of my personal policy that my desk remain cluttered enough that no one could ever look at it and know exactly what I was up to.

"Yep. How was your niece's party?" I looked up so she could see the concern radiating from my expression. It was part of a covert language we shared allowing us to engage in two conversations at once. There was the discussion the rest of the world heard and the meaning that only the two of us understood. For the sake of our listeners at nearby desks, I added, "You went to the party, right?"

"Of course I did! I forgot your gift, though." There was a slight uprising to one side of her lips that let the rest of the world know she felt guilty. It told me she appreciated the sentiment, but that now was not the time to talk about all of what was happening with her.

I started working again. "I saved my plane ticket and receipts in Portland in case I have to prove my whereabouts to Susan. Not that I don't trust you to relay simple messages convincingly."

"No offense taken. I saw Cassie at the party. She named her kids after things people put on food."

Cassie and I never liked each other. Ironically, that was who Lindsey was with when Lindsey and I met. "Like what?"

"Pesto."

I laughed and tried to picture her now. "She always liked to eat. Did she get fat?"

"No. She married a chef though."

"Makes sense. You guys catch all the way up?"

"We're not much of friends anymore." Lindsey looked even worse than she did a few seconds ago. I knew they weren't in close touch anymore, but I never got the sense that there was a rift between them. I asked, "Why? What happened?"

Lindsey was dismissive. "Just girl stuff."

I didn't know what to say to that, so I just made a noise of acknowledgement. Even though we had trained in martial arts together and I was confident in her ability to defend herself, the combination of her recent tears and her lunch with a man she was planning on marrying forced me to question, "That little bump on your head? Anything to do with your migraine?"

"Sort of. More girl stuff."

Lindsey looked away. Her claim of a migraine was related somehow to her problems, but there was no narrowing of her eyes that would have indicated that her new man hit her. I relaxed a little.

Still looking off around the office, Lindsey said, "So I'm deep in it over sending you guys to Portland for nothing. Rodrick's got my back, but New York is pissed."

I tensed right back up. "Well, it was the person New York sent us that made the trip irrelevant."

"I'm sure they'll field the blame if I mention that to them."

The egos and stupidity that stood in the way of meaningful work drove me crazy at times. "I know it doesn't matter to them, but it had to be said."

I barely caught Lindsey's thanks because Rodrick's door opened and Jackie stormed out of it looking like she wanted to stab someone. Lindsey gestured her head in that direction, rolled her eyes and walked away.

I jumped out of my chair, threw my sketchbook on my desk and made for Rodrick's office before anyone else could take his time away from me.

He had circled around his desk and was a yard away from his door when I blocked it and asked, "Do you have a few minutes? I need to talk to you about an urgent development."

The look on his face suggested that he didn't have a few minutes, but he told me, "Come in. Close the door." He turned, walked back to his desk and leaned against it rather than going back around it to sit down. He folded his arms across his chest.

"I have a showcase for a major record label that requires travel. I need to leave like, now to catch my flight, I can be back by 10 tomorrow morning. In the meantime, the last of the motion graphic package for Circle Velocity is rendering now and will be done within the hour and all of my other active projects are on the shared drive in case something changes in my absence, but are within range of their target date of completion if things remain quiet."

He had the look of a man whose day was growing harder with every new moment. "Now isn't the best time for this."

"I didn't choose this opportunity."

His brow furrowed. A year ago, the job for Senior Account Manager had gone vacant. Rodrick wanted me for the job and told me as much before the job was announced. The New York office wanted Lindsey and made it clear to Rodrick that anyone not happy with that choice could leave.

Feeling bad for me since he felt I had deserved the job from the dues I'd paid, Rodrick offered to do whatever he could to aid me in my music career. It was a consolation prize that helped me be supportive of them passing over me for Lindsey because at the time, I was really angry at the way the events unfolded.

Because he was a man of his word, even when it became inconvenient, that second place prize meant him accommodating things like me leaving early on a moment's notice to fly to Colorado to showcase for a label.

"Where are you headed?" He asked.

"Charlemagne, Colorado. I'm flying into Denver and driving from there."

"Take some of the field recording gear. Get me some sound elements that we can build into our sound effects database for the science fiction movie we'll be pitching next week. Make sure none of the sounds can be placed distinctively outside of a 75-mile radius of this building and expense nothing associated with leaving California. Is that all?"

"Yep."

"All right. Go on then. Good luck."

He followed me out of his office and went for the elevators. I went back to Supply and checked out a portable recorder, some cables and a stereo microphone with wind guard. After that, I grabbed a few essentials from my desk, took my luggage and headed for the elevators myself.

"Where are you going?"

I turned around to find Jackie chasing me down.

"Rodrick wants me to do some field recording for our sound library. It's for our pitch to Emblem Entertainment next week."

"I thought your car was at your apartment."

I tried to keep my anxiety hidden. "I'm having a friend who owes me a favor pick me up."

She muttered something and waved me off. I quickly departed and made it downstairs right as my cell phone rang. "Are you out front?" I asked.

"I am for another 15 seconds." I heard a car honk in the background and Truck tell the person who honked where they could go.

"I'm here." I hung up as I crossed the threshold to the street. Truck was parked right in front of the building, blocking a lane because there was no parking in front of our building. He waved a middle finger at me. I blew a kiss at him and threw my luggage in the back seat. I kept my laptop bag and the case with the field gear with me in the front seat.

After we were underway, he asked, "So this is it, huh? You gonna big a big rock star now?"

"Only if things go according to plan," I said while trying to adjust my bag and the case so that I wouldn't be so uncomfortable.

"So all is forgiven about your apartment?"

"I used to have a temper too."

Truck gave me a look that lasted long enough for me to check the road ahead of us in case we were about to hit something. "If you say so." He said and resumed looking ahead.

"Say it," I told him.

"I just don't think this is gonna work out the way you think. That's all. You're putting yourself way out there."

"Maybe it won't work. I'll live easier if I try and fail than the other way around. What if I stay home and she signs a deal and becomes a big star? I don't want to live with that. I'd rather her fail with me than she succeed without me."

"Sounds like you're decided." Then there was that awkward silence that always accompanied our agreeing to disagree all the way to the airport.

He did wish me luck as I got out of his car and I thanked him. It was more than I expected from him because he didn't think in terms of artistry and expression. He believed that being an adult simply broke down to getting a job that allowed you to make a living and maybe travel someplace nice every now and then. Having purpose and passion behind how you made that living wasn't part of the equation in his world.

My world was ruled by the types of sacrifices art demands. Long hours of seclusion. Investing large sums of money to meet artistic goals so that what I put out in the world met my expectations. Sleeplessness. Forgetfulness...

I was through security and at my gate by the time I realized that I hadn't told Lindsey a thing about this. It also occurred to me that she was keeping her own secrets from me. As much as I liked to think that our relationship wasn't permanently affected by her getting the Senior Account Manager job over me, maybe that wasn't true for either of us.

I considered calling her, but knew it would just

be more awkwardness and I didn't want any more of that in my day.

As if on cue, we were warned of a flight delay. This time due to the snow in Denver. I texted Tessa to ask if there was anyone who could pick me up from the airport because I'd never driven through heavy snow before.

I was 37 pages into the novel I bought in the book store after clearing airport security before my phone notified me of an answer.

"They're exaggerating. It isn't as bad as they say. Rent a four wheel drive. You'll be fine," She texted back.

Her reassurance was somehow depressing. I put my phone back in my pocket and emitted a huge yawn. Out of fear of missing my flight if I fell asleep, I got up, changed into my 'ready for snow' layers of clothing in the men's room and walked around the terminal until they finally called us to board. Thankfully, we were only a half hour behind. Once on board, I fell into a dreamless sleep while the plane was still taxiing to the runway.

***

Denver got off to a bad start. The first five rental car agencies I went to had sold out of four wheel drive vehicles. "I have an all-wheel drive Ford Escape if you want that?" The guy behind the counter of the sixth rental car agency offered.

"Didn't I just ask for that?"

"No. You asked for a four wheel drive."

"The last I checked, Escapes have four wheels, so an all wheel drive would use four wheels. Or is my math off?"

He had the look of someone who wanted to call me things that would get him fired. "Look, Sir. The two terms are not interchangeable. There are fundamental differences between four and all wheel drives that will take me just long enough to explain, that the Escape will likely get rented to someone else during that span. However, if you're willing to cease attempting to insult my superior knowledge on this topic and take the car, I can say that it is your next best bet in lieu of a four wheel drive vehicle." He raised his eyebrows in question and poised his hands over his keyboard as if he knew I was an idiot, but not so big of one as to let the Escape go to someone else to prove a point.

He was right. "I'll take it."

"I thought so," was so prevalent in his smug expression, that he might as well have said it.

"That little speech you gave me. Is that a script they have you memorize or were you freelancing?"

He didn't answer.

***

The drive up to Charlemagne was slow. Scary, and painfully slow once I exited the interstate highway and began traveling on US Route 6 and then US Route 24. Both of the routes snaked through the pitch black Rocky

Mountains except for where my headlights were pointing.

Unlike my usual self, I was extremely conservative with the gas pedal as I drove and slid over the combination of snow and ice. I made it to Charlemagne in one piece, however. As I drove in to the town proper, I became a lot less tense and allowed myself brief glimpses of sight seeing. The homes all seemed to be two stories with lights randomly shining from behind closed drapes in some of them.

We were supposed to perform at the town's bowling alley and to get there, Tessa told me to stay straight on the main road and then I'd run into it. She was right, but the place seemed dead from the outside.

I parked, grabbed the case with the recording equipment in it and went into the bowling alley. My heart sank in my chest immediately. There were exactly two people in there. One was putting bowling shoes in their numbered cubbies and the other was cleaning the floors. Feeling utterly dejected, I went to the shoe rental counter and asked the guy behind it when everyone left.

"They shuffled out about ten minutes ago. They're setting up at Olivia's house. You the guitar player they're waiting on?"

"Yeah. Who is Olivia?"

He looked at me like I was stupid. "Tessa's mom."

He told me Olivia's house was the end house closest to the bowling alley in the second row of homes down from the main road I had just come in to town using. I thanked him and found a set of stone steps peaking out from the snow descending to the street in front of Olivia's row of houses.

The street lights provided dim, but adequate light to get down the steps, but I slipped and nearly fell from a patch of ice on one of them. I thanked Truck for packing my insulated boots and trudged down the rest of the way in the snow where I had better footing.

As I came around the front of the house, I could see through an uncovered living room window that the ground floor of Olivia's house was packed with people. A stereo was playing loud enough for the rumble of bass guitar and kick drum to ooze into the crisp nighttime air.

The front door was unlocked, so I let myself in. There were a good twenty people in the living room. I wove through them and put the case of recording equipment down by the microphone stand, acoustic guitar and P.A. System that had been set up in a corner of the room. No one knew where Tessa or her mom were, but someone suggested I try upstairs so I bound up them two at a time. The hallway and all the rooms were dark except for one. I was close to calling out and announcing that I had arrived, but something told me not to.

I approached the crack in the door with a sudden, unexplained caution.

There were three people in the room. I recognized Tessa saying, "...be here soon. I don't know why I need him here anyhow, it isn't like you're signing us both. Anyone can play guitar. Let me just hire someone and let's move on with our lives."

It felt like I was suddenly clued into something every single naysayer in my life already knew - success would always elude me. I would never be anyone's first choice. Not Tessa's, not Razor[Gun]'s, not Lindsey's.

I had punched the wall next to me and started towards the stairs before I knew what I was doing. Behind me I heard someone ask what the noise was a few seconds before Tessa called my name. I could hear her curse and a few seconds later, follow behind me.

As I was making my way down the stone steps I had seen a park bench off to the side of the stone steps leading to the row of houses beneath Olivia's row. I sat on it with the intent of calming down before going back into the house to get the case from Razor[Gun] that I was responsible for, but forgot.

Not a minute later, Tessa was sitting next to me.

"I told you when we first met I'd eat my own young if it would make me famous and rich. Why would anything I do surprise you?" Tessa said, patience radiating from her every word.

She never told me anything like that and I told her so. She just kept breathing and looking at me, her exhales making mist in the frigid night air. When she broke the silence again, her voice was tight with anger. "I'll pay you. $500. That should make us square. So how about it?"

"No."

She let out a frosty sigh, then waited while glaring at me. When I didn't move or speak, she said, get your butt in gear and let's go play this gig. You can cry about this after."

To keep my fist from bloodying her mouth, I turned my body away from her and I looked off in the direction of the snow-covered woods that surrounded Charlemagne. The smell of Aspen was thick in the air.

There was a brief thunder in my ears as a freezing gust of wind swept across my face. When I turned back to face her, the noise from the wind died down enough for me to hear the approach of footsteps crunching in the snow. They stopped at what I guessed was a few feet behind me. I heard the sound of a bullet being racked into the chamber. I didn't have to look to know who was back there, or who the gun was pointed at. There was a part of my brain registering that I should be scared, but fear never persuaded my behavior when anger was part of the conversation.

"Oh, come on...you going gangsta now?" I mocked, "Shooting me won't make you rich and I'm not important enough for it to make you famous, you'll just be in jail for awhile."

"Go. In. The. House. And. We'll. Settle. This. Later." Tessa warned through clenched teeth from beneath the fur lined hood of her parka. She brushed some of her long dark curls back from across the side of her narrow face and hooked it behind an ear. The ends still cascaded down the front of her. I could only see one of her eyes from this angle.

"Or your mother will shoot me," I finished for her,

then turned to her gun toting mom. "Judging by how you apply your makeup, I have serious doubts how well you can see." Then I stood up and headed for Olivia's house. Her mom said something in Spanish behind me that probably expressed disappointment with me not staying seated long enough for her to shoot me.

I heard the crunch of Tessa's and her mother's boots trailing after me towards the house. I let the door close behind me after I came in and heard someone answer their angry knock after Tessa and her mom realized that I had locked the door as I entered.

It didn't delay them long, but it was enough time for me to push through the throng of guests, grab the case and be on my way out as they entered.

"Where do you think you're going?" Tessa demanded, looking at the case, then shifting to my face.

"Well Lordy be Massa, I don been freed now. I'sa gonna catch me a flight home." I replied, then pushed past them through the door.

"Mom!" Tessa complained.

"You know what will happen if you don't turn around right now!" Olivia screamed.

"Bite me," I yelled.

Tessa and her mom weren't the only ones who followed me outside. A few of the guests were coming out to see what the commotion was about. I could hear multiple people ask what was happening as I made my way around the front of the house and started up the stone steps back to my car.

Tessa screamed something in Spanish.

There was a sharp crack that quieted all the voices at the same moment I felt a strong punch in my lower back.

I spun with an elbow strike. To face my assailant. To hurt him. No one was there.

I slipped, and on my way to the ground, everything slowed down enough for me to see Olivia pointing the gun at me and then everything went black.

Lindsey Falco
Monday, 18 December 2006

It was fifteen minutes into Lindsey's day before she realized that she recognized her husband's car in the dream. It belonged to Malcolm Price, a guy she had gone out with the previous month.

They had met at a book store skimming through the new release section. She had picked up a book he had just finished reading and after he told her how good it was, they got to talking and before they parted, had exchanged phone numbers.

A single phone call later and they were out on their first date. It was one she wouldn't soon forget.

Unlike other guys she had gone out with who took her out to movies and dinner on first dates, he opted to take her to a modern dance performance by the Barbara Branch Dance Company at the Music Center in Los Angeles. She had never been to a dance performance before, but thought it might be nice to see how 'cultured people' enjoyed their evenings. It also didn't hurt that Malcolm warned her that the dress code was casual. She didn't need to buy a gown or anything like that.

The performance itself had moved her with an intensity that she didn't anticipate. Along with the waif-like dancers she expected, were a few larger dancers carrying normal body weight and the way they moved…Lucy could feel the varying intensities in their physical intonations. Even now, the power in the gesture as one of the dancers pulled up her right hand into a fist as if to say, "Yes, I will fight you if I must." was imprinted in Lindsey's mind. Somehow, it made her need to move in expression of her deepest held beliefs.

Lindsey felt a gratitude towards Malcolm for introducing her to this.

After the show, still feeling the rush of emotions the performance brought out in her, she followed Malcolm's lead as they walked around the area, meandering through narrow walkways between the liquid flowing silver steel lines of a nearby concert hall as they arced towards the stars above. She found it easy to simply bask in his words as he spoke about growing up in Chicago.

The walk took them across the street, past the entrance to The Museum of Contemporary Art. As they passed, he told her about one of the exhibits that was currently on display, then confessed to being a museum slut. She had never heard the word slut used in such a way before and thought he was kind of clever. She made a mental note to use the word similarly in the future. Perhaps, people would think the same of her.

Their walk brought them into a breezeway with long rows of planters ringed with tall, narrow trees running down the center of it. Here, in the half-light spilling from the windows of the buildings flanking them, he held her hand and her heart swung with the wide sweeping movements of their combined grasp.

The night continued, just this side of magic until it

was time to leave. When they got to Malcolm's car, he realized he had lost his keys. The expression on his face at this discovery shocked her out of her feelings of safety. He looked like a person who was very, very scared and didn't know what to do next.

She gave a circumspect glance around the parking lot while Malcolm stood paralyzed. She walked around to his side of the car and looked on the ground by his feet and under the car.

"I must have dropped them." He said finally. Lindsey chose not to answer that. She was beginning to get irritated with Malcolm and could see that she was going to have to take charge of the rest of the evening if they were to get home safe.

Lindsey came around the car and looked through the driver's side window to see if the keys might be in the seat or if she could see them on the floor. Coming up empty, she went back around to the passenger side of the car and looked through that window to see if the keys might still be in the ignition, but there was no sign of them.

"Do you think maybe you dropped them in the theater?" Lindsey asked.

"I don't know." Even Malcolm's voice had changed. It was scared and small.

Lindsey watched him guardedly. "I better backtrack where we've been." And he set off in the direction they entered the parking lot.

For the first time that evening, Lindsey noticed the

damage her cute shoes where doing to her feet. She suggested that they call for help, but he had already walked far enough away that she would need to probably jog to catch up to him. When he didn't respond to her call for him to wait, she grudgingly followed after him.

They backtracked their entire date through every alcove and across every street where they crossed earlier until they were all the way back to the closed doors of the theater and found nothing. He wondered aloud if they might be in the trash that the night-time cleaning crew threw out, but the expletives from Lindsey that answered the query made Malcolm think better of rummaging through trash. Finally, Malcolm called his roommate to come get them. It was two in the morning by the time he arrived to pick them up.

When they parked in front of Lindsey's apartment building, Malcolm sheepishly asked Lindsey to let him make it up to her, but by this time she was so angry and tired, there was nothing she could think of that he could do to atone for how their evening ended.

He called a few times and left messages over the next week, but she couldn't get those last few hours of their date out of her mind. The cynical part of her told her that was the real Malcolm that she saw, not the witty, knowledgeable and confident guy she started the date with, but maybe she was wrong and maybe the dreams were wrong too. Perhaps it was worth another shot.

Lindsey picked up her cell phone, found Malcolm's number in her call log and pushed the button to dial it. It was a lot earlier in the morning than she would normally call someone, but she felt like the rules were meant to be broken under the circumstances. It went to voicemail. "Hey Malcolm, it's me, Lindsey. I'm sorry it took me awhile to get back to you, but I hope you don't hold it against me. Things have been a little crazy on my end, but I was hoping we could get together on another date sometime soon." Lindsey gave him her phone number again in case he grew tired of waiting on her and had deleted it. She hung up, got dressed and got herself to the building Razor[Gun] kept its LA offices in.

Right as she was walking through the metal detector at the security gate access area for the building, her phone started ringing. The security guard waved her on through and she quickly grabbed the phone out of the plastic bucket she placed her metal belongings in and answered it without looking to see who it was. "Hello?" There was a sniff, then, "Is this Lindsey?" The woman's voice on the other end of the line was ragged.

Before answering the question, Lindsey pulled the phone away from her face to see whose name showed in the caller ID and saw Malcolm's name. Don't tell me he's married and I'm about to faceoff with his wife, she thought to herself. She put the phone back to her ear. "Yes. This is Lindsey. How may I help you?" As the words left her mouth, Lindsey felt foolish and small and cursed her phone etiquette training from work.

"Hi. My name is Martha...Malcolm's mom. I don't mean to disturb you, but you left a message on his phone for him to call you?"

There was a pause. Lindsey waited for Martha to say more. When she didn't

Lindsey prompted her with a, "Yes?".

"I'm afraid, my son is no longer with us."

"I'm sorry. What did you say?"

There was a pause on the other end of the line. Lindsey could hear sniffling, then with one huge burst of emotion Martha blurted into the phone "He's dead, my son Malcolm is dead." and followed her pronouncement with a series of sobs and wails so powerful, Lindsey couldn't help but visualize them wracking Martha's body. Lindsey stood motionless.

"Excuse me, miss? I'm afraid you're going to have to take your things and move on through." The words seemed to slowly embed themselves in Lindsey's mind and she looked at the security officer who uttered them with a blank stare, uncomprehending.

The officer repeated "Please take the rest of your belongings and continue out of the way so other's can get through." Lindsey nodded, still silent with the phone pressed up against her ear. The officer gently took her arm by the elbow and led her around the X-ray receiving table to clear the aisle for other employees to pass through the security area. "Are you okay miss?" The officer asked. "Do you need me to get you something? Water, maybe?"

Lindsey stood still and unresponsive long enough for the officer to think maybe his question didn't register when her head slowly turned to him and said, "No".

The word felt distant to her, as if it hadn't come out of her own mouth.

She could still hear Martha crying on the other end of the phone.

She waited.

When Martha again gained control of tears, and apologized, all Lindsey could manage was, "How? When?"

"Pills. Pills and alcohol. Last night, the coroner said. His roommate found him this morning."

"I...I'm sorry. I don't know what to say. I'm stunned."

"Me too. I mean, I didn't see any signs of this coming at all and I don't know how I missed them. I keep trying to tell myself that he put on a strong face for my benefit, but I can't make myself believe it. I can't stop blaming myself."

"You shouldn't do that Ms..." Lindsey let the word hang, not sure what to call Malcolm's mom.

"You can call me Martha, child."

"Okay. Well, Martha, you shouldn't blame yourself. Malcolm was a great guy full of culture and he could only have turned out as sweet as he was by having such a loving mother and upbringing. He was easily the best date I ever went on."

"Thank you. Thank you for that. I better go, young lady. I have much to do and many phone calls to make. Did you plan on attending the funeral? Should I text you the viewing and funeral arrangements?"

"Yes. Please."

"Okay. I'll do it from Malcolm's phone." There was a break in Martha's voice. "That way you'll know who it is from. I'm glad we had a chance to talk, Lindsey. It's made me feel better. Bye now."

"Goodbye Martha. I'm sorry for your loss. He was a great guy."

Lindsey bought herself a coffee at the newsstand in the lobby before taking the elevator up to the Razor[Gun] offices. The whole time, she wondered how wonderful life might have been if things had worked out and she had become a member of Malcolm's family.

In her own family, Lindsey managed to mend most of the rifts, but between her and her older sister, she was the wild one. Lindsey spent her spare time going from one boy to another, while Susan had remained steady with her boyfriend from the age of 16 through graduation. Within a year of graduating, Susan and her boyfriend had married and a year later, had their first child. Though no one had come out and told her any-thing directly, Lindsey had always felt a small divide between her, her sister and her mom. There was a level of responsibility that they had obtained, that she hadn't.

With Malcolm, there seemed to be an attraction and acceptance that even though it was a single date, held the distinct possibility of becoming something life-long. Speaking to his mother only reinforced her feelings that she had just missed out on something spectacular. As she hung up, Lindsey wished that she would have had a chance to get to know Malcolm better.

185

Lindsey still didn't know what to make of the news she just received as she exited the elevator into the Razor[Gun] reception area. The receptionist, Laney Ramsay was on the phone and gave her a wave. Lindsey, waved back and continued on into the back offices and straight to her office.

Normally, she would have spent some time in the break room having breakfast and coffee with some of her officemates, but today, she needed space to try and figure what she was feeling. She had her quiet for twenty minutes.

"Hey Lin. What's with the hermit routine? You too good for your peons today?"

Lindsey looked up to see Liam Thatcher leaning in her doorway and Eva Lautner standing next to him.

"Yeah, what's with the 'tude…dude?" Eva added.

"Look. She even outsourced her coffee." Liam said to Eva, then turned back to Lindsey. "I guess you'll be replacing us next, huh?"

"Hey guys. I'm not feeling that good today."

"Have you tried kicking someone? That always makes me feel better."

Liam suggested.

"What!? No. Why does your answer to everything involve kicking?"

"It works." Liam said.

"Remember that guy I went out with a week or two ago?"

Both Eva and Liam nodded their heads.

"He committed suicide."

Eva wore a serious expression, but asked, "You're kidding, right? That isn't funny."

The haunted expression on Lindsey's face answered her question.

Eva asked, "When did this happen?"

"I guess some time last night. His mom called and told me this morning." Eva's expression changed. Now there was doubt.

"What do you mean his mother called you?"

"I mean, she called me."

"How many times did you go out with this guy?"

"Once."

Eva crossed her arms in front of her chest. "And after one date, you're close enough to his family for his distraught mother to call you and inform you that he committed suicide. How did she get your number?"

Lindsey caught the gist of what Eva was getting at and her eyebrows raised in a mix of anger and hope. There was definitely no wedding ring tan on his finger. She made sure to get a good look during their date.

"She called from his phone." Lindsey looked down at her desk thinking. "Do you think maybe it was a jealous girlfriend? Or maybe it's just some other girl that he's dating?" Even as she asked the question though, in her heart, she knew that wasn't the case. She could feel that whoever was on the other end of the line was telling the truth at least about that. "Look. Let's talk about this later. Okay? I have to get this pitch figured out in spite of my lack of ability to concentrate at the moment."

Lindsey was able to put in a solid three hours of work when the phone rang on her desk. She checked the caller ID hoping that it might be Malcolm while knowing it wouldn't be. It wasn't.

Lindsey picked up the line. "Hey Laney, what's up?"

"There's someone here to see you." Laney sounded bored.

"See me? Who is it?" Lindsey asked. She could hear Laney ask the person and then back into the phone she said, "It's a surprise, but you'll want to come out."

"Are those your words or my visitor's?"

"Hers. Come out already, I have stuff to do besides be the liaison between you and your visitors."

"Okay. I'll be right out."

Sitting in the lobby of Razor[Gun] was a Black woman who looked to be texting on her cell phone. She wore a black dress that hugged the curves of her body and showed a good amount of cleavage. She looked to be about 50 years old, but in impressive physical condition and extremely pretty. She had the kind of presence that filled the room. Even though there was someone else in the room sitting down, Lindsey almost tripped over his feet before noticing him. Lindsey looked the question at Laney and Laney nodded that she was the person. As Lindsey approached, the Black woman stood up and put her phone in what looked like a gem-encrusted handbag Lindsey guessed cost half her annual salary. She was taller than Lindsey.

She must be at least six feet tall, she thought to herself.

"Hi. Lindsey?"

Lindsey stopped where she was a few feet shy of being in arm's reach. "Do I know you?" Lindsey asked.

"I'm Malcolm's mother. We talked this morning."

There was a resemblance between the two, especially around the eyes and mouth. "Okay. But I don't understand why you're here." Lindsey offered.

"After our talk this morning, I thought about what you said about blaming myself, and it really helped. I thought I'd take you out for lunch and get to know you better. After all, you and Malcolm seemed to really have the beginnings of something beautiful based on what he told me about you." Lindsey brightened a bit at the thought that Malcolm had talked about her to his mother, then it quickly faded when the next thought reminded her that he was dead.

"Please, Lindsey." Martha remained composed for the most part, but in her eyes was a plea bordering on something Lindsey couldn't read. "I feel like if we can talk some, it might give us both a little more closure."

"Okay." Lindsey said. "There are still a few things I need to do before I leave though. Do you mind waiting? It shouldn't be more than 20 minutes." Lindsey knew that she could have left that very moment, but wanted to see how interested this lady truly was in having lunch with her.

Martha's smile never left her face. "Why, of course I can wait. My whole afternoon is free."

Lindsey smiled back. "Great!" She said with faked enthusiasm. "I'll be back in a jiff." Then Lindsey quickly departed back into the Razor[Gun] offices. She found Eva in one of the editing bays.

"She's here." Lindsey told Eva in an excited whisper. Eva looked up confused and whispered back. "Who is here?"

"Malcolm's mom. She wants to take me out for lunch so we can talk and get some closure." Lindsey bent down to one knee so that she would be about eye level with Eva. "I told her that it would take me another 20 minutes to get to a good break off point in my work, but it didn't phase her one bit. What do you think I should do?"

"Are you sure it's his mom?"

"I didn't ask for I.D., but she looks old enough and resembles him a bit."

"Did she say how you're supposed to provide closure for her?"

"She said that based on what he told her, it sounded like we had something special."

"That date sure sounds a lot different now than the day after you had it."

"Do you think I don't know that?" Lindsey demanded.

"I don't know. Do you want me to crash the party? I can just try and tag along, or follow you guys and go to where you go and be available if you need me. Just text me the address and I'll be there. I'll even bring Liam, just in case."

"Follow then."

"Alright. I'll let Liam know and don't give her an opportunity to slip anything in your food or drink. She might be crazy and out to get you for some reason." Eva thought about what she had just said. "Not that I'm paranoid."

"Got it."

Lindsey went back to her desk and worked while waiting for another 15 minutes to pass.

Martha insisted on driving, so Lindsey relented with a warning on the elevator that she would need to be back at her desk within an hour. Martha seemed unfazed by the time constraint and told Lindsey that she had a reservation for them at a nearby restaurant and that she called ahead to let the host know that they were running a little late. When Lindsey asked which restaurant, Martha told her that she wouldn't have heard of it anyhow, so wait and be surprised.

They arrived on the street to Martha's illegally parked Aston Martin DB9 Coupe waiting directly in front of the entrance to Lindsey's building. There was a parking ticket on it. Lindsey watched Martha pull the ticket from under the windshield wiper of the car without any noticeable irritation and stuffed it absently in her purse.

"I guess if you can afford a car like this, a parking ticket is no bother at all, huh?" Lindsey asked after ducking into the vehicle. She realized that it was a rude thing to say, but too late. The words were already out there. Martha let out a small laugh and pulled into traffic without looking.

A horn sounded behind them along with an expletive. Martha's smile grew a bit and she weaved in and out of traffic with a pace and an abandon that Eva couldn't have hoped to keep pace with. She shuddered as she realized that she was on her own.

At the restaurant, two valets greeted the car. The valet on Martha's side slipped into the driver's seat once she was clear of the door. The other valet welcomed Lindsey with a cheerful, "Welcome to Cylinder." He took her hand and helped her out of the car.

Above the front door, the Cylinder sign hung suspended by four one-inch thick metal cables and was made of what looked to be hammered brass. As they approached the door, a young man in a black suit and gold tie left his post behind the host's podium and unlocked the door. As he opened it, he welcomed them both, but Martha by name. I have your table right over here as requested Ms. Price, then led them through narrow walking rows of empty tables.

"I hope you don't mind sitting at a proper table with normal chairs. Sitting in booths bothers my back."

Lindsey's, "No problem," for an answer was by reflex. She was engrossed at the lavish sight of the restaurant they were in. Everything was LED lights reflecting off of brass cylinders and through purple, red and gold fused glass decorations. Everything in the place stunk of money, but there were no customers. "Is this place open?" Lindsey asked Martha.

"Well, yes and no. This is the restaurant version of a pop up store. I know the owner. The place is all set and will open tonight at seven PM and stay open 24 hours a day for seven days. He owes me a favor, so I was able to get us afternoon reservations before even the movie stars get a taste of what his executive chef has planned."

"Wow," Lindsey said, awed by how much control Martha seemed to have over her world. She wondered briefly why Malcolm never mentioned this about his family, but then, why would any guy until he knows the girl isn't a gold digger. Lindsey knew for a fact, that she could definitely get used to living like this. She was so amazed at this new experience, that she forgot all about being nervous that Martha drove so fast and recklessly, there was no way for Eva and Andros to follow them without being found out and even if they did follow, the restaurant was closed to all but her and Martha.

"Don't worry dear," Martha told her, "I'll have you back at your job within the hour and order anything you like, don't worry about the price. Jacob, the owner owes me big time."

Lindsey looked at the menu and paid attention to it for the first time.

The appetizers began at $50. "Are you sure?" Lindsey asked.

"Live it up, girl. This place is going to be gone soon and this special menu with it." Martha leaned back into her chair and perused the menu. Her purse chimed and she bent over the side of her chair to pull out her phone and excused herself as she did so.

After she greeted the caller, she told the person that she was having lunch and would be in the office in another hour and a half. She paused to listen and then told the other person to call her if it became necessary, but only as a last resort. She hung up, excused herself once more saying that she needed to update something in her calendar and began rapidly pressing buttons. Lindsey turned her attention back to the menu. When she had decided, she set her menu down.

Martha's menu was already on the table and asked. "Decided?" After Lindsey nodded yes, Martha summoned the waiter with a wave of her hand. He had been waiting patiently near the door to the kitchen. He took their orders and disappeared.

After they had ordered, Lindsey tried to settle in and relax a little bit, but she was still on edge. She had felt off center ever since her dream about Melanie being kidnapped and since then, things had begun moving very fast in her life. "How did you know where I work?" Lindsey asked.

"I Googled you, dear. You really ought to see what information you have floating around on the Internet if you want to stay private."

Lindsey looked down feeling stupid to not have thought of that. She resolved to do some online searches on herself once she got back to the office. When she looked up, Martha was looking at the restaurant's decor. She looked like she hadn't slept much since Malcolm's death. "This place is modern and all, but why does modern always have to feel so cold?" She asked.

Lindsey looked around with a more critical eye. "The colors are kind of warm though. I wouldn't decorate my apartment like this, but I don't mind it in this small a dose."

"You work for a design firm. What would you do different?"

Lindsey didn't answer immediately. She had already established the look and theme of the restaurant in her mind, so she closed her eyes, imagined for a few minutes and answered, "I would have fewer tables and arrange them slightly off of a diagonal from one another so the sight lines were better. I think it would give the room the feeling of more space and make the patrons feel more like they are able to be seen since it seems to me that is a large part of what the attraction to this place will be."

"Good observation." Martha remarked, then leaned in towards Lindsey like she was about to reveal a secret. "I like the way you think. You seem to get things. Most people would see no room for improvement or shrug their shoulders and ask me my thoughts." Martha leaned back in her chair and looked up wistfully. "You must have had some amazing conversations with Malcolm. He used to always surprise me with his creative intellect. Did you ever see any of his drawings?"

Lindsey shook her head. "No." She said a bit more demurely than she had intended.

"My boy. I guess knowing Malcolm I should have guessed that you didn't spend much of your time together talking. He loved women with a peculiar passion even as a child."

Lindsey flushed when she realized what Martha was getting at and corrected her. "No, Martha. It wasn't like that." Beneath the thin layer of offense she felt, Lindsey couldn't help but wonder if Malcolm was the gentle, caring man she had a tragic date with, or a womanizer like his mom described. They didn't seem to know the same person at all.

Martha gave Lindsey a measured look. "Well, it's over now regardless of what it was, isn't it?" Martha picked up the wine glass the waiter had set down while they spoke, closed her eyes, drank deeply, then continued. "You know I still haven't been able to bring myself up to gathering his things out of his apartment. His roommate would like me to take care of it in the next day or two, but how do you pack the things from your dead son so easily?"

Lindsey said that she didn't know.

"He shouldn't complain though. I'm paying Malcolm's share of the rent until I can gather myself and get over there. I just can't bear the thought of having someone else do it for me. I'm his mother. It should be me."

"I'm truly sorry for your loss Martha."

"Tell me, please." Martha had a pleading in her voice that finally sounded like the damaged woman on the telephone. "Tell me about your last conversation with my son."

Lindsey answered before thinking and said, "Our last conversation, wasn't really a conversation." In her mind, Lindsey was playing back the horrible irritation that she felt at Malcolm even as she knew that she would eventually forgive him. She thought that she would just make him suffer for a short while-teach him a lesson.

"What do you mean, dear?" Martha asked.

Lindsey realized that it was probably not in her best interest to tell the person who drove her to the restaurant and was paying for her meal what had actually happened the last time her and Malcolm spoke, but like it or not, she had a guilt about it too large to lie her way around it.

"I was mad at Malcolm the last time we spoke."

Martha said nothing. She looked haggard like she had some kind of emotional hunger that was quickly growing into starvation.

Lindsey continued. "We had gone on a date to a dance performance and he had lost his keys at some point during the night, but he didn't discover that until it was time to drive me home for the evening. We ended up backtracking our entire date with me in a pair of high heels only to never find them. He called his roommate to come pick us up which he did and Malcolm spent the entire ride home apologizing, but I wasn't ready to forgive him yet. After that night, he called me three or four times but I didn't return his calls. I haven't told anyone this, but the last one, he sounded real broken up and desperate for me to call him back, but I didn't until it was too late. That was when you got my message, called me and told me what happened. I can't help but wonder if by not taking his calls, I contributed to his suicide."

Tears had streaked gently down her cheeks as she told Martha about her last moments with her son, and it surprised Lindsey how reserved she had been while telling the tale. She half expected to burst into sobs, but there was relief there too. She needed to tell someone what had happened and now that it was out, she might be able to find some peace.

The plates of food arrived at the now silent table. Martha looked at her food and Lindsey looked at Martha. She was waiting for Martha to curse and blame her for Malcolm's death. Perhaps it wouldn't be right, but on some level, Lindsey felt like she deserved it.

Martha picked up her fork and began eating. The rest of lunch not another word was spoken between the two. Lindsey suspected that she said the wrong thing, but wasn't sure how to rectify any animosity Martha was feeling towards her. This was supposed to be about closure and you only find that through truth, but she must have miscalculated, she thought.

Once their meal was finished and they were ushered back into the car, Martha turned on the radio and blues music wailed and moaned to break the silence until Martha pulled up in front of Lindsey's building.

As Lindsey got out of the car, Martha told her, "Thank you." and then drove off.

Lindsey returned to her job feeling a bit melancholy. When she got to her desk, there was a note taped to her computer monitor that read, "I'm back at my desk. Come see me." It was signed A.K.

She got up and found Andros at his desk uploading files onto the shared drive while drawing in a sketch book. On his desk were a few rough drawings of "Wanted" poster for the Everain beer campaign.

"So that's the new campaign, huh?" She asked pointing at the posters.

"Yep. How was your niece's party?" Andros stopped working and looked up at Lindsey. "You went to the party, right?"

"Of course I did! I forgot your gift, though."

Andros started working again. "I saved my plane ticket and receipts in Portland in case I have to prove my whereabouts to Susan. Not that I don't trust you to relay simple messages convincingly."

"No offense taken. I saw Cassie at the party. She named her kids after things people put on food."

"Like what?"

"Pesto."

Andros laughed. "She always liked to eat. Did she get fat?"

"No. She married a chef though."

"Makes sense. You guys catch all the way up?"

"We're not much of friends anymore." Lindsey shifted her weight uncomfortably. Part of her wanted to tell Andros about the impact her date with Malcolm had on her, her dreams about Melanie and her lunch with Martha, but the part that didn't had control of her mouth. "Why? What happened?" Andros asked.

Lindsey shook her head. "Just girl stuff..."...like she

got married, had children and doesn't seem to be running from anything in her life like I am. She finished in her head.

Andros hmmmm'ed a noncommittal noise. "That little bump on your head? Anything to do with your migraine?"

"Sort of. More girl stuff." Lindsey turned her gaze away from Andros and looked past the Razor[Gun] staff into a future that looked lonely and disappointing. "So I'm deep in it over sending you guys to Portland for nothing. Rodrick's got my back, but New York is pissed."

"Well, it was the person New York sent us that made the trip irrelevant."

"I'm sure they'll field the blame if I mention that to them."

Andros stopped working and looked at Lindsey. "I know it doesn't matter to them, but it had to be said."

Lindsey forced a laugh and thanked him. She searched for an excuse to peel herself away from Andros, but came up with nothing that didn't sound contrived. Then Jackie did her first favor ever for Lindsey and came out of Rodrick's office. Lindsey motioned her head in that direction and Andros jumped out of his chair and nearly ran into Rodrick's office. He was inside with the door closed a moment later.

Once back in her office, Lindsey managed to make sure all of the pieces for the Von Conor pitch the next day were in order and ready to go, then she did a test run-through with the team she was pitching the idea with in the conference room, and as near as she could tell, everything was green lights and gas pedals. The feeling of success not being far away was contagious. She kept a fast pace for the rest of the work day and by the time she left for home, she could feel herself slowly getting a handle on her emotions with the aid of work as distraction.

"I'm going to be okay." She said out loud as soon as she shut the front door of her apartment and the sound of her voice comforted her. She walked into her kitchen, pulled out a bottle of Cabernet and poured herself a glass. A few minutes later, she had a piece of salmon in a pan over fire. She could hear the people who lived next door on the living room side of her apartment moving around. They had a nine year old that was a sheer terror when it was time for him to do homework in the evenings.

Through the wall, the call and response of his mother's yelling and his cries continued like normal and Lindsey figured that there was another 15 minutes left of their verbal battle left before he'd settle in and do what he was supposed to when she heard what sounded like a tall piece of furniture being knocked over and slamming into the floor.

That boy is enough to make a person swear off kids forever, she thought. She took a long, soothing sip of wine.

Even though her meeting with Malcolm's mother shook her up at first, she figured at least that part is over.

"My mother isn't done with you yet."

Lindsey let out a small scream. It was Malcolm's voice, but it didn't come from inside her head. It sounded like it came from her bedroom, where now, she realized the sound of something falling also came from. Her neighbor's apartment was silent.

"Malcolm?" Lindsey called. She moved to the edge of the kitchen and she stopped, leaning the upper portion of her body into the living room. The door to her bedroom was across the living room and near the far wall, so that all she could see was the open door swung into the bedroom and light shining on it from her nightstand lamp. Did I leave that light on, she thought to herself not trusting that to be her normal habit suddenly.

"Malcolm? Are you here?" She had heard of people who were haunted by the recent dead.

She waited in that same position watching the bedroom door to see if a shadow passed across it and listening for any more noise to come out of the room, but nothing happened.

Smoke from her burning salmon broke the spell and she quickly ran back to the stove, grabbed the handle to the pan and threw it into the sink and turned the tap on over it, creating a cloud of steam, hoping that she caught it in time for the smoke detector to not register what just happened.

Her nerves where still taut and even though she knew it would do no good against a ghost, she reached into the silverware drawer and grabbed a knife for each hand.

On the way back to her bedroom, she flipped on the ceiling lamp in the living room. The switch was near her front door. "Malcolm? If you're here, talk to me."

She waited.

No sound.

She looked back at her front door and as quietly as possible, she released the chain from the door and unlocked the deadbolt in case she had to make a quick exit. She would only have to turn the handle.

She thought of how some people say they could feel a presence in a room sometimes, but Lindsey felt nothing. She became very aware of every shadow the ceiling lamp threw. Thankfully, she thought, her place was small enough that most of her furniture was tucked up against walls. There was nothing standing free in the middle of the room for something to hide behind until she was near it.

Her heart was beating so intensely in her chest, she instinctively looked down to see if she could see her chest rise and fall with the cadence, but she couldn't. She came up to the door along the wall that gave her the best view of the bedroom. The creaking floor betrayed her approach.

Still, there was no sound coming from the bedroom. No movement. She closed the last few feet of distance between her and the slightly open door.

She took a peek through the gap between the door and the door frame where the hinges were. No one was hiding behind it. She pushed the door all the way open.

The room appeared as she had left it from what she could tell.

She lowered herself to check under her bed, but the bed skirt blocked her view. She'd have to get close enough to lift it to see beneath it.

She got down on both knees. Waddled on her knees to the bed, so that if someone were beneath it wielding a blade, their closest clear target would be her thigh, not her Achilles.

When the bed was barely in reach, she bent over using the extra few inches of one of her knives to lift the bed skirt. There were shoe-boxes and two low profile storage bins looking to be in the same dust covered position she had left them in. Not able to see clear through to the other side of the bed from beneath it, she raised back up and walked to the far side of her bed.

No one was there.

I heard something fall in here though, she thought and remembered the closet. She walked back around her bed to where her sliding closet door shared the same wall as the bedroom door and gathered herself for a moment with a couple fingers on the handle. She pulled on it with her left hand and backed up at the same pace it opened, staying a little behind the sliding closet door with the knife ready in her right hand. When the door wouldn't go any further, she crouched down and knife leading the way, leaned her head in the closet to see the parts of it still closed off behind the sliding door.

Everything was as she had left it.

There was no indication as to what she heard fall in her bedroom and this realization triggered the memory of a visit she made at the age of nine to see her mom in the hospital.

She and Susan had been driven to the hospital by their next-door neighbor Ms. Becker who they were staying with while their mom was sick. Lindsey had been to the hospital before to visit her dad shortly before he died, so she was extremely worried about her mom. Susan tried to calm her, but Lindsey couldn't be pacified. When they arrived at a locked door that they were told her mother was behind, she was told that she was too young to enter.

"I'm sorry, dear. You have to be at least 12 years old to go in there." The lady at the counter told her.

Lindsey threw a tantrum, but her behavior didn't gain her entry.

For the next three years her mom was in and out of the locked ward in psychiatric hospitals from multiple attempts at suicide.

By the time Lindsey was eighteen, her mother had stabilized and gave off the appearance of normalcy. She thought it was as good a time as any, to ask her mom why she used to keep trying to kill her self.

"It was your dad, child. He always had those sweet words to make me do whatever he wanted and he wanted me to join him."

"But he was dead." Lindsey told her trying to make sense of it.

"I know," her mom answered, "but he was still talking to me and he was very convincing."

That conversation struck a fear in Lindsey so powerful that she sabotaged every relationship that threatened to put her in her mother's position. It wasn't worth the risk to her after seeing the torment her mother endured for years.

That was the real reason she had sabotaged everything with Malcolm.

It was all for nothing, though.

Malcolm was dead, but he was still talking to her.

To be continued...

If you liked *The Gospel of Wolves Ep. 1,* you'll LOVE what happens next.

To make sure you don't miss it, register using the link or QRCode below:
www.chriswesley.com/TGoW_Join

ACKNOWLEDGEMENTS

A VERY SPECIAL THANKS goes to my Beta Readers who subjected themselves to the first public draft of this book as my editors. They cleaned up my grammar, cited typos and told me when I was muddling up the story. Of course, the final draft is my own creation, so if you found any mistakes, it's my fault. Not theirs. In order of their volunteering, a merry round of cheers goes to:
Corinne Diaz, Lanetta Singleton, Winston Widdes, Vesta Javaheri, Anne Hall and Katlin Sweeney.

A VERY SPECIAL THANKS also goes out to everyone who voted for the cover of this book. In no particular order and regardless of which cover they voted for another merry round of cheers goes to:
Aaron Graper, Winston Widdes, Steven McGill, Miena Eggleston, Alana Wong, Maggie, Kim, David Cohen, Melissa Dinwiddie, Norval Watson, Marion Duke, Rebekah Nemethy, Debra Renfro, Ronnie, Frank Srubar and Jenny Dome.

LAST, BUT NOT LEAST, THESE ARE THE PEOPLE who had some form of impact on the making of this book. At least the one's who would recognize me by name in a line-up. Pat Wesley, Tim Sweeney, Deborah Kolodji, Susan Dobay, Pam Creel, Just Kibbe, David Cohen, Mom, Dad, Melissa Dinwiddie and Tah Phrum Duh Bush

ABOUT THE AUTHOR

Chris Wesley was eight years old, the first time he caught the attention of a crowd with his story-telling. Seven children stood captivated as Chris told of the time when the family's pet Doberman Pinscher became engaged in a horrendous fight with his father, ending with his dad killing the dog with a knife. It was fifteen minutes long and a lie. But then, fiction is like that.

Since that day, Chris has written music reviews and a music business column for Night Moves Magazine, acted in independent movies and plays; wrote, cast, directed, shot and edited an independent short movie, started bands and gone solo. He plays a few instruments and has generally been what some politely call "a wise guy". That means he says things, he probably should have kept to himself. He does this often. But then, smart asses are like that.

He is the creator of The Wilderness, a transmedia storyworld where artists, businesses and technology face off in a new frontier of ever changing paths to success every bit as dangerous and unpredictable as the wilds first traversed by early American settlers. In it, he gets to write fiction, say things he shouldn't, create visual art and record music that pop radio would likely crap on if given the chance. He has fun with this. But then, independents are like that.